A loud noise _____ _____ ck, and April's head banged agu____ e window.

Clay jerked the steering wheel. Another crack came out of the night. The back window shattered, raining glass down on April's head. The truck squealed and the back wheels made it fishtail on the road.

"What happened? What did you hit?" She focused on Clay's profile.

His jaw tensed. "I didn't hit a damned thing. Someone's shooting at us...and he just got my tire."

Clay wrestled with the steering wheel. It took all the strength he had to keep the truck on the asphalt—and he had to. If he swerved onto the shoulder, the truck could flip or skid out to a stop. They couldn't stop. Whoever shot at them wanted to disable the vehicle. Wanted them to be stranded in the desert.

"I see headlights. They're coming after us..."

EVASIVE ACTION

CAROL ERICSON

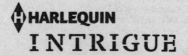

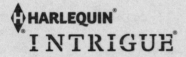

ISBN-13: 978-1-335-13653-4

Evasive Action

Copyright © 2020 by Carol Ericson

Recycling programs
for this product may
not exist in your area.

This edition published by arrangement with Harlequin Books S.A.

For questions and comments about the quality of this book, please contact us at CustomerService@Harlequin.com.

Harlequin Enterprises ULC
22 Adelaide St. West, 40th Floor
Toronto, Ontario M5H 4E3, Canada
www.Harlequin.com

Printed in U.S.A.

Carol Ericson is a bestselling, award-winning author of more than forty books. She has an eerie fascination for true-crime stories, a love of film noir and a weakness for reality TV, all of which fuel her imagination to create her own tales of murder, mayhem and mystery. To find out more about Carol and her current projects, please visit her website at www.carolericson.com, "where romance flirts with danger."

Books by Carol Ericson

Harlequin Intrigue

Holding the Line

Evasive Action

Red, White and Built: Delta Force Deliverance

Enemy Infiltration
Undercover Accomplice
Code Conspiracy

Red, White and Built: Pumped Up

Delta Force Defender
Delta Force Daddy
Delta Force Die Hard

Red, White and Built

Locked, Loaded and SEALed
Alpha Bravo SEAL
Bullseye: SEAL
Point Blank SEAL
Secured by the SEAL
Bulletproof SEAL

Her Alibi

Harlequin Intrigue Noir

Toxic

Visit the Author Profile page at Harlequin.com.

CAST OF CHARACTERS

April Hart—For the second time in two years, April has run out on a wedding—but this time the jilted bridegroom is a dangerous drug dealer on a mission. Now she must return to the first jilted bridegroom for protection.

Clay Archer—This border patrol agent had his heart broken when his fiancée called off their wedding weeks before the event. When she returns to his life, she brings enough danger and baggage to send his protective instincts into overdrive.

Adam Hart—April's brother has had his share of tragedies, and he uses them to keep his sister on his side for his next wild scheme.

Jimmy Verdugo—A small-time drug dealer playing a big-time game, he's not going to allow his errant bride to disrupt the biggest deal of his life.

El Gringo Viejo—The nickname of a man reputed to be a drug supplier in Mexico, he's also reputed to be April's missing father.

Chapter One

The snowy-white tulle of April's veil rustled as she climbed out the window. Her satin shoes landed in the moist dirt with a squishy sound. She yanked the frothy concoction from her head and stashed it behind a bush.

She took a deep breath and peered around the corner of the house, her curls falling over one shoulder. The stretch limo gleamed in the morning sun of New Mexico, and she shivered. The car looked more like a hearse now—her hearse. Who said New Mexico was the land of enchantment?

Narrowing her eyes, she chewed the strawberry-flavored gloss off her bottom lip. If she fled in the limo, it could be tracked, but at least it would solve her immediate problem of no funds. She considered creeping back through the house to retrieve her purse, but she valued her life too much—at least someone did.

How far could she get barreling down the highway in a stretch limo? Way too conspicuous—sort of like this wedding dress.

She patted the lace bodice of one side of her dress to make sure she still had the strange wooden disc she'd found in Jimmy's desk, and then drew out her cell phone from the other side. She tapped the icon for the car app loaded on her phone and smiled at the little dots on the map—her saviors.

She called up a car, and then strolled to the front gate, although her feet itched to break into a run. This couldn't be a clean getaway, not with Jimmy's security at his beck and call, but nobody suspected a thing at this point. She could play the blushing bride for another ten minutes. Hell, she'd played at being in love with Jimmy for the past six months.

Oscar, the guy working security at the front gate to Jimmy's estate, jumped to his feet. "Getting cold feet, April?"

"Just jonesing for a smoke. I know how much Jimmy hates cigarettes and I'm trying to squeeze in a few before I quit for good." She pinched the low neckline of her gown between her fingers and adjusted it. "You have one I can bum?"

Oscar's gaze followed the movement, his eyes widening for a second. "I—I do."

"That's what I'll be saying in an hour. I'd really appreciate it…and I'll step outside the grounds so Jimmy won't know a thing." She put a finger to her pouting lips. "You know I'm good at keeping secrets, don't you, Oscar?"

Oscar's face reddened, obviously remembering the time she caught him rummaging through Jimmy's desk, and he scrambled for a cigarette in his front pocket. "I know that, April, and I appreciate it."

He shook a cigarette free from a crumpled pack and held it out toward her.

Sliding it from the pack between her index and middle fingers, she said, "Thanks. Got a light?"

He flicked his lighter, and she leaned in to touch the end of the cigarette to the flame.

She waved the cigarette at the gate. "I'll just slip outside to enjoy it, and if Jimmy happens to smell it on me… I didn't get it from you."

"Of course not, thanks." He lunged for the gate, probably happy to get her out of his sight before she could get anything else on him to report to his boss.

Holding the cigarette in one hand and the skirt of her dress in the other, she stepped outside the gates of Jimmy's compound. She traipsed down the drive to the street, her breath coming in short spurts. Her gaze shifted from side to side. She'd better not bump into any guests arriving early for the nuptials— Jimmy's guests.

Once she turned a corner and got clear of Oscar's sight, she dropped the cigarette and crushed it under the toe of her shoe. Then she pulled out her phone again and texted Adam. The wedding is off. Don't come near the estate. Don't go near Jimmy.

The phone buzzed in her hand, and she answered the call from the app car on its way. "Hello?"

"I'm about a block away in a blue Honda. Big houses here. Can I get in the gate?"

"I'm outside the gate. I'll be waiting on the sidewalk. Hurry."

"Uh, okay."

Two minutes later, a Honda pulled up to the curb. April checked the license plate, compared the driver to the picture on her phone and jumped in the back seat. "Go!"

The driver's bugged-out eyes met hers in the rearview mirror. "Where am I going?"

"The nearest bus stop. Wait." Her fingers creased her satin skirt into folds. How could she buy a bus ticket? She had no money. No wallet. No credit cards. She'd be a sitting duck at any bus stop for Jimmy and his so-called business associates. Now she understood why he always had an entourage. *Idiot.*

"Keep driving." She pounded the back of the driver's headrest. "I'm thinking."

"Are you running away from your own wedding or something?" The driver adjusted his glasses and punched the accelerator.

"Yes." She reached into the front seat and grabbed his arm, turning his laugh into a snort. "What's your name?"

"Jesse."

"Jesse, I have a deal for you." April tugged at the diamond ring on her left hand. "I'll trade you this ring for your car."

Turning his head, he squinted at the ring cupped in her palm. "Nice rock, but I can't do it. I need my ride to make money. This is the only job I have."

She slumped back in her seat. She could pawn the ring for cash, but that meant she'd be wandering around Albuquerque in this damned dress.

"My friend Ryan might be down, though."

"Really?" She shot forward again. "Where's Ryan?"

"He lives about ten miles from here. He's trying to sell his car, and he might take that piece for it instead of cash."

"Perfect."

She waited until Jesse hit the highway. Then she buzzed down the window and chucked her phone outside. She wouldn't be able to contact Adam anymore, but Jimmy couldn't trace her whereabouts.

Thirty minutes later, the trade with Ryan went smoother than she expected, and he even threw in a hundred bucks, cash, to seal the deal.

She rolled up the money and wedged it into her new car's cup holder. She scooped the wooden token pressed against her breast from the bodice of the dress and dropped it in the other cup holder. Running her hand across the dashboard, she yelled out the window. "No GPS?"

"Does that car look like it has a GPS?" Ryan shoved his hands in his pockets. "No refunds."

"I'm not looking for a refund." She cranked on the engine of her new vehicle. "Just point me in the right direction for the 25 south."

Jesse strolled to the car. "You going to Mexico?"

"Maybe." She leveled a finger at him. "You remember the rest of our deal, right?"

"Yeah." Jesse's Adam's apple bobbed in his skinny, razor-burned neck. "If anyone asks, I picked you up and dropped you off at a bus depot in the city."

"That's right. The 25?"

Jesse gave her directions and she sped off, leaving the two young men gaping in her rearview. After her first burst of speed, she eased off the gas pedal. She didn't have her driver's license with her, and Ryan's name was on the car registration. She didn't need any trouble. Her impulsiveness had gotten her into enough trouble.

The car had enough gas to get her out of Albuquerque and almost down to Hatch Valley, just over the halfway point to Juarez. She could lose herself in Mexico, do a little investigating, too, even though it sure seemed as if Jimmy had contacts south of the border.

She wouldn't be the first of her family to disappear in Mexico.

After about three hours on the road, April pulled into a gas station just out of Hatch and dashed into the convenience store. She grabbed a diet soda and smacked thirty bucks on the counter.

"As much gas as this will get me on pump number five, less the cost of the drink."

The female clerk nodded, eyeing her from the top of her poofy hairstyle to the tips of her satin shoes, peeking out from the hem of her wedding dress. "Are you going to the wedding or coming from it?"

"On my way. It's a beautiful day to get married, isn't it?"

"Uh-huh." The clerk popped her gum and rang up the purchase with her long, violet fingernails.

April pumped the gas, waved to a little girl giggling in the car next to hers and plopped onto the driver's seat, gathering yards of billowing material inside after her.

She continued south, heading for Las Cruces. Just another ninety minutes or so, and she'd be across the border. She didn't have any ID with her, but that never stopped people in the know from slipping into Mexico undetected. Her gaze shifted to the side, taking in the signs for the 10 west and Tucson. One hour to Mexico. Four hours to Tucson.

"Ah, hell." She veered toward the ramp that would take her to Arizona.

She had enough gas. The weather couldn't be beat. She didn't know anyone in Mexico. And when could she ever resist Clay Archer?

CLAY ARCHER SWATTED at the fly buzzing around his face and gritted his teeth as the sound of the young Border Patrol agent's retching finally subsided. He'd been there, done that. No shame.

The agent, Rob Valdez, straightened up, wiping his arm across his nose and mouth. "D-do you think the head's in the tunnel?"

Clay spit onto the desert floor. "We'll find out soon enough. You wanna go back to the truck and get some water?"

"No." Valdez squared his shoulders. "I gotta see what's in the tunnel."

"You might not like what you see." Clay squinted through his sunglasses at the mound of sand and dirt that marked the end of an underground tunnel between Arizona and Mexico.

"I gotta get used to it. You're used to it." Valdez rubbed his eyes and replaced his sunglasses and hat, flicking the stiff brim with his finger.

Clay took a step closer to the headless woman at his feet, one arm flung to her side, the other crossed over her body, the fingers of her hand curled. His nostrils flared as he crouched beside her, avoiding the blood-soaked dirt with the tips of his boots.

He reached for the woman's hand, cold and stiff across her lifeless body, and pried open her fingers. Between his own thumb and forefinger, he pinched the object clutched in her hand and pulled it free.

"What is it?" Valdez hovered over him, the smell of vomit, sweat and fear coming off his body in waves.

"Do not upchuck on the body."

"I'm done with that." Valdez took a few steps back, as if not sure of his own statement.

"It's a calling card." Clay held up the housefly carved from wood, almost as realistic as the ones swarming the dead body. He waved it in the air.

"Las Moscas." Valdez glanced over his shoulder as if expecting members of one of the most murderous drug cartels in Mexico to come riding up on ATVs. "Why would they do this to one of their own mules? And a woman?"

The pile of dirt at the tunnel's exit shifted and one hand clawed its way out of earth like a scene from a horror movie. They didn't need movies—they had their own, real-life horror.

Clay stepped around the young woman with care as if she were sunbathing in the desert instead of missing her head. By the time he reached the tunnel, it had already spit out half of Nash Dillon's body.

Dillon scrabbled out the rest of the way, empty-handed. He yanked the mask from his face and coughed. "Nothing. No head. No drugs."

Valdez let out a noisy sigh. "Agent Archer found something in the dead woman's hand."

Dillon raised his brows as he brushed the dirt and debris from his green uniform.

Clay cupped the wooden carving in his palm and held it out to Dillon. "This is the work of Las Moscas."

"Not surprised." Dillon tipped his head toward the woman. "Only a few reasons why I can think of that the cartel would kill one of its own mules—she double-crossed them, screwed up somehow or started working for us."

"She's not one of ours." Clay held up his hands, the wooden token held between two of his fingers. "As far as I know, we've never used a woman."

"Don't lie, Clay." Dillon clapped his hat back on his head and wiped his designer sunglasses on the hem of his shirt. "The DEA uses wives and girlfriends when they can get them on board—or when they've been wronged by their drug-dealing spouses or tire of the lifestyle."

"That's DEA, not Border Patrol." Clay squinted into the harsh desert light. "We've got company."

The two other agents swiveled their heads in unison toward a caravan of trucks and SUVs accompanied by a cloud of sand and dust.

"Hope there's a coroner's van among those trucks." Dillon stamped the dust from his boots, jerking his thumb toward the body. "They need to get this young woman out of here. Give her a little dignity, regardless of the mess she made of her life."

The trucks and law enforcement personnel brought a flurry of activity with them. The local PD in Paradiso wouldn't conduct the homicide investigation, as it was too small to have a homicide division—not that the department didn't see its share of murders along this stretch of the border.

The Pima County Sheriff's Department would take over the thankless job of investigating the murder, but as usual with drug crimes, there would be no evidence, no witnesses and a bunch of nameless, faceless suspects.

Clay studied the men and women going about the business of investigating a headless corpse in the desert, and he took a swig of water from his bottle.

"Crazy business."

"What's that, Archer?" Espinoza, a homicide detective for the sheriff's department, looked up from his phone and squinted at Clay.

"Nothing. Just thinking about the insanity that goes on in this town."

Espinoza spread his arms wide. "Paradise, right?"

"Yeah, some clueless gringo even got that wrong, didn't he? *Paradiso* doesn't even mean *Paradise* in Spanish."

"Wrong name—" Espinoza kicked at a pile of sand "—and wrong description."

Clay and the other Border Patrol agents packed it in, and left the scene to the coroner and the homicide detective. On the way back to his truck, Clay poked Dillon in the back. "You taking some time off?"

"Heading to a rodeo in Wyoming. Can you hold down the fort?" Dillon swept his hat from his head and tossed it onto the passenger seat of his truck.

Jerking his thumb over his shoulder, Clay said, "Unless we find the head or the drugs, especially the drugs, there's not much for me to do on this one."

"The drugs will be on the street by the time I come back." Dillon nodded toward the new agent, hanging back, the green around his gills matching his uniform. "You think he'll work out?"

"He'll be okay." Clay leveled a finger at Dillon. "I remember your first dead body. You didn't do much better."

Dillon scooped his hair back from his forehead and flashed his white teeth. "I guess you're right."

"Don't break that pretty face riding one of those

bulls." Clay turned and strode to his truck with Valdez waiting by the passenger side.

"You getting in or staying out here?"

Valdez's eyes bulged briefly. "Just didn't want to sit in the truck without the AC. Is that it for the day?"

"That's it for my day. You're gonna go back to the office and write up this report. Make sure you check in with the sheriff's department to see if you can add anything before you send it to the Tucson Sector."

They both climbed in the truck, and Clay cranked on the air. They'd gone several miles before Valdez turned to him, clasping his hat in his lap.

"Do you think they'll find the head? What do you think Las Moscas did with it?"

Clay raised his stiff shoulders. "I don't know. Don't think about it too much, kid. It'll make you..."

Clay drilled the desert horizon with narrowed eyes. He didn't finish his warning to Valdez because he didn't know what it made you. What had it made him? Bitter? Hard?

He blew out a breath. The work hadn't done that.

A half hour later, Clay pulled his truck into the parking lot of the Paradiso Border Patrol Office—one of several offices in the Tucson Sector.

For the most part, the residents of Paradiso chose to remain blissfully ignorant about the dangers at the border. The violence of the drug trade didn't affect them directly, so they were able to carry on with their daily lives—despite people meeting bloody ends several miles down south.

Livestock, lettuce and pecans had been kind to the folks of Paradiso. Its close proximity to the tourist trap of Tombstone hadn't hurt, either. They lived in a bubble. There hadn't been a murder within the city limits since…Courtney Hart.

Clay left Valdez in the office and swung by Rosita's to pick up a burrito on his way home.

As he slapped his cash onto the counter, Rosita put her hand on his. "We heard news of a body at the border."

Once the Paradiso PD was involved, news traveled fast. He couldn't blame them. The residents had a right to know—whether they cared or not.

"Unfortunately, that's true."

"Drugs?" Rosita's dark eyes shimmered with tears, and a knife twisted in Clay's gut.

Rosita's youngest son had gotten hooked on meth—it hadn't ended well.

"Yeah, probably a mule."

"A girl?" She clasped her hands to her chest. "We heard it was a girl this time."

"A young woman, yes. Ended up on someone's bad side." He shoved the money across the counter. "Keep the change, Rosita."

"Is there a good side when it comes to drugs?" Rosita swept up the bills. "Thanks, Mr. Clay."

He waved and reached for the door, stepping aside for a couple of customers coming in for dinner. He tossed his bag of food on the passenger seat and took off for home.

His house lay outside the collection of the newer developments that had sprung up in response to the pecan-processing plant. He preferred a little space between him and the next guy.

As he turned down the road that led to his house, he loosened his grip on the steering wheel and flexed his fingers. He swung into the entrance to his long driveway and slammed on the brakes to stop behind an old, white compact sporting New Mexico plates.

His muscles tense, he reached for his weapon wedged in the console and waited in his idling truck. The individual Border Patrol sectors were small enough that the bad guys could discover the identities of the agents if they had a mind to. He held his breath as the driver's side door of the car swung open, and a...bride stepped out.

Clay whipped the sunglasses from his face and hunched over the steering wheel. Damn, that was no bride. That was bridezilla—April Hart in the flesh.

Leaving his weapon in the truck, he shoved open his door and placed one booted foot on the dirt and gravel of his driveway. He unfolded to his full height, straightening his spine and pinning April in a stare.

She tossed a mangled mane of blond hair over one shoulder and offered up a smile and a half-raised hand. "Clay, it's good to see you."

Did she expect him to rush to her and sweep her

into his arms? He folded those arms across his chest in case they got some crazy notion to do just that on their own. He dipped his chin to his chest. "April."

She dropped her hand and tugged on the top part of the dress that clung to her slender waist and rose to encase the swell of her breasts. "I suppose you're wondering what I'm doing here…in this dress."

"You took a detour on the way to our wedding two years ago and you just found your way back?" His lips twisted into a smile while a knife twisted into his heart.

"N-no." She clasped her hands in front of her, interlacing her fingers. "It's a long story. Can we talk inside?"

"Do you ever have any other kind of story?" Before she could answer his rhetorical question, he dipped back into his truck and swept his bag of food from the passenger seat and holstered his weapon.

He slammed the door of the truck and stalked up his driveway, brushing past April in her wedding finery.

The gravel crunched behind him as she followed his footsteps. "Someone left you a present. It was here when I drove up."

A round, pink-striped box sat on the corner of his porch. Clay tilted his head to the side, his pulse ratcheting up a notch. Nobody left him presents—especially the kind in pink boxes.

"You have your hands full. I'll grab it for you." April barreled past him, the crinkly material of her gown skimming against his hand.

A spike of adrenaline caused him to make a grab for her dress, but she slipped through his fingers. The story of his life.

"April, wait."

"That's okay. I got this." She reached the porch and grabbed the ribbon on the top of the box. "This is heavy."

She lifted the box a few feet in the air. Then the lid came off and the bottom of the box hit the porch with a thud.

April's scream reverberated in his ears as the severed head bounced once, splattering her white dress with blood, and rolled off the porch.

Chapter Two

April opened her mouth to scream again, but the sound died in her throat, which seemed to be closing. She gurgled instead, falling back against the wooden railing of the porch, her hand still clutching the pink ribbon, the lid of the hatbox swinging wildly and flinging droplets of blood throughout the air.

"Oh my God. It's the head." Clay pointed to the soggy hatbox tipped on its side. "Don't touch that."

Her gaze darted to his face. Was he out of his mind? Why would she touch that box again?

She dropped the lid and swallowed. "It—it's a severed head."

"I'm sorry you had to see that." He pulled a cell phone from the front pocket of his green uniform shirt. "I'll get someone to pick it up."

"I would hope so." Her hands clutched at the skirt of her dress, until she noticed the streaks of blood marring the white billows. She dropped the material and folded her arms over her midsection.

"You don't seem surprised. You called it *the* head. You know that head?"

"I do, although I didn't expect it to show up on my porch. I didn't expect *you* to show up on my porch, either." He started talking on his cell phone and held up his key chain, jingling it in the air.

She nodded and he tossed the keys at her. She caught them in one hand and opened the door to his house—a house and home that could've been hers.

She set the keys on a table by the front door. Closing her eyes, she took a deep breath and let it out slowly. Nothing with Clay could ever be uncomplicated. There had to be a head in a pink hatbox sitting on his porch the very day she decided to drop in for a visit.

Her eyelids flew open. Was that what she was doing?

Her gaze traveled around the room. He hadn't much modified his manly space...or his habits. Everything had a place. Even the pillows on the couch sat erectly and in order.

April sauntered to the couch and flipped one of the pillows on its face. She scanned the framed pictures on his bookshelf, looking for her face in vain.

She jumped as a siren wailed on its way to Clay's house. A few minutes later, what sounded like a hundred vehicles pulled up outside. She peeked through the blinds at the uniformed officers swarming Clay's driveway. The head obviously had something to do with Clay's work as a Border Patrol agent. He'd been almost more surprised to see her on his doorstep than the head in the box.

She crossed her arms, cupping her elbows, as a shiver zigzagged up her spine. Clay played a dangerous game down here at the border. Although part of the Tucson Sector, the Paradiso Border Patrol Office was small and everyone—including the drug dealers—knew the agents. Had someone left that head as a warning to Clay?

Good luck. Clay would always do his duty.

The door burst open, and her heart slammed against her chest.

Clay stuck his head into the room. "Detective Espinoza wants to talk to you for a minute."

April smoothed the skirt of the dress with shaky hands. "Is the head still on the driveway?"

"It is, but they're going to bag it soon. I'll ask the detective to come in here, if you want."

"I'll be all right as long as I stay on the porch."

He pushed the door wide, and she swept past him, the dress crinkling between them.

April stepped onto the porch, lifting her skirts to avoid the cone that had been placed next to the stain of blood where the box had sat.

A gray-haired Latino in a suit and a cowboy hat stuck out his hand, his eyes widening as they dropped to her dress. "Ms. Hart, I'm Detective Espinoza. Agent Archer told me you're the one who picked up the box and it had been here when you arrived."

"That's right." She took in his rugged features

and frame from the top of his black hat to the tips of his silver-toed boots. He hadn't been one of the cops in Paradiso or one of the Pima County detectives during her family troubles.

"What time did you arrive at Agent Archer's house?"

She glanced at Clay from the corner of her eye. "About five o'clock."

"The box was already on the porch?"

"It was."

"Did you see anyone around the house when you got here?" His gaze flicked again to the wedding gown and then back to her face.

"Nobody." She snapped her fingers. "The dog. Clay, where's Denali? Do you still have him?"

"Of course I still have him." He lifted one eyebrow. "He's staying overnight at the vet."

"Is he okay?"

Espinoza cleared his throat. "So, you didn't see or hear anything unusual when you drove up to the house. Did you get out of the car?"

"I didn't get out of the car. I was tired from my drive and put the seat back to take a nap. Clay got here about an hour after I did, waking me up when his truck pulled in behind me."

"Why did you pick up the box?"

"Clay had his hands full." She shrugged. "Does it matter?"

Espinoza narrowed his eyes. "Hart. You're the daughter of C. J. Hart?"

April's pulse skittered and jumped. "I am. Does *that* matter?"

"Just asking." He waved his pencil up and down the dress. "Why the wedding gown?"

"I just came from a wedding." Her jaw tightened as Clay shifted beside her.

"We're going to want to test that blood on the dress. Did it come from the head?"

"I picked up the box by the ribbon on the top, thinking it went all the way around the box. It didn't. When I picked up the box, the lid came off in my hand and the box fell. The…head bounced out and splattered the dress, and then I dropped the lid."

Espinoza clicked his tongue. "That's a shame."

"Not really." She tossed her wilting curls over one shoulder. "I can rip a piece of the fabric out right now, if you like."

"No hurry. Based on what Agent Archer told us, we're pretty sure we know what happened here."

Another truck squealed up to the scene and, in the glare of the spotlights, Nash Dillon jumped out of his vehicle and hovered over the authorities transferring the head into a bag.

When they finished the job, Nash strode to the porch. "I guess we found her head, but damn, left on your porch? They're thumbing their noses at us, bro."

Clay shook his head. "I need to get some cameras at my house. I didn't even have Denali here to sound the alarm."

"Oh, hey, April." Nash raised his hand and continued his conversation with Clay, as if the appearance of Clay's ex-fiancée in a blood-spattered wedding dress made all the sense in the world. But then Nash Dillon had always been about Nash Dillon.

When the medical examiner's van pulled away, Detective Espinoza handed April a card. "You can drop off the dress anytime in the next few days."

"I'll do that." She snatched his card and spun around to the screen door, leaving Clay and Nash talking shop.

She paced the floor a few times, and then plopped down on the couch, grabbing one of Clay's perfectly placed pillows and hugging it to her chest. What was she doing here? That poor woman's severed head must be some kind of omen. She should've never shown up on Clay's doorstep. Should've never run to him for…what? Why did she come to Paradiso? Clay Archer had been the only bright spot for her here.

She couldn't recreate the magic they'd shared. She'd destroyed that, taken a sledgehammer to it.

The door opened and Clay stepped into the house, sweeping the hat from his head and unbuckling his equipment belt. His weapon clunked against the kitchen counter as he set down the belt.

"What a crazy day." He dragged a hand through his dark hair, which made it stick up in different directions. He held up the bag that contained his dinner and swung it from his fingertips. "I kinda lost my appetite. You want it?"

She stuck out her tongue. "No, thanks. Who was that woman?"

"Probably a drug mule who double-crossed Las Moscas. We found her body earlier, just outside a tunnel running across the border." He braced his hands against the counter and hunched forward. "Are you really interested in this?"

Her fingers dug into the pillow. Las Moscas? He had no idea how interested.

"How do you know it was that gang, Las Moscas?"

"Cartel. Drug cartel and we know because the people who murdered this woman left their calling card in her hand."

April swallowed. "A fly?"

Clay's eyebrows jumped to his hairline. "How'd you know that?"

Shrugging, she schooled her face. "Las Moscas. The flies. I mean, not like a real fly, right?"

"Well, there were plenty of those." He glanced up at her face, and his jaw tightened. "Sorry. They left a carved, wooden fly in her hand."

April jumped up from the couch and tripped over the wedding dress. She made a grab for the back of the couch to stay upright.

"Are you all right?" Clay had taken a couple of steps closer to her, his brow creased.

"I'm okay. Like you said, it's been a crazy day." Her words stopped him in midstride.

He blew out a breath and shoved his hands in the pockets of his green pants. "Do you want to tell me what this is all about, April? The wedding dress? Coming to Paradiso? Adam isn't here, is he? Is he in some kind of trouble?"

Oh, yeah, her brother was in all kinds of trouble, but he could get into trouble anywhere. It didn't have to be Paradiso—where all their trouble had started.

"Adam isn't here and I'll be happy to tell you all about this—" she plucked at the dress "—but I'd like to change first, if you don't mind. Detective Espinoza wants this dress, anyway, or at least pieces of it."

Clay's head swiveled as he took in the room. "Do you have a suitcase in your car?"

"No. I don't have a bag with me. I don't have anything with me." She linked her fingers in front of her, holding her breath. If Clay tossed her out on her rear, she wouldn't blame him.

Clay rolled his eyes. "All right. I have a pair of sweats you can probably use, and help yourself to a T-shirt. I'm gonna have a beer. You want one?"

"Sounds good." She pointed to the hallway that led to his bedroom. "I'll be right back."

She slipped into his room and closed the door behind her, leaning against it and closing her eyes. She didn't have to worry about a wife or a girlfriend. She'd kept tabs on Clay the past few years. She shouldn't be happy that he'd remained single, but he always would have her heart. Ridiculous to think she could blot out the memory of Clay with someone like Jimmy—no matter how much Jimmy had seemed like Clay…at first.

She hadn't known just how ridiculous until this morning—her wedding day.

She reached around and tugged at the zipper of the dress. She shrugged out of the straps, and the gown slipped from her body, pooling at her feet.

The shimmering white strapless bra and the lacy panties had to stay. She stepped out of the satin pumps and over the heap of material resembling a small mountain of foam on the floor.

She rummaged through Clay's dresser and snagged a pair of army-green sweats with the Border Patrol insignia on the left thigh. She paired the sweats with a white T-shirt from a 10K in Tucson and tiptoed into the living room on bare feet.

Clay hadn't moved from the kitchen counter but now sat perched on a stool, hunched over his phone and a second bottle of beer.

"I'm going to have to do some catching up." She pinged his empty bottle with her powder-pink-tipped fingernail.

He shoved the other bottle toward her. "Haven't touched it."

"Are you sure you don't want it?"

"I probably need a clear head for what's coming." With his foot, he nudged the other stool in her direction.

Hitching up the legs of the sweats, she sat down and grabbed the beer. She raised the bottle. "Here's to catching the SOBs who murdered that woman and defiled her body."

"The particular SOBs? Probably not, but we're working night and day to bring down Las Moscas." Clay scratched at the damp label on the empty beer bottle. "That wedding dress?"

April took a long pull from her beer and squared her shoulders.

Clay's cell phone buzzed next to his hand and he held up one finger. "Hold that thought. I'd better get this."

How much should she tell Clay about Jimmy and the whole mess? She'd never even told him why she ran out on their *own* wedding—and she never would.

"You sure Adam's not here?" Clay held up his phone.

"Of course." She squinted at the call coming through and pressed a hand to her chest. "Why is Adam calling you?"

Clay lifted a shoulder and answered his phone. "Adam?"

He paused for a few seconds and then held out the phone to her. "He wants to talk to you."

"Me?" April's fingers curled into the soft cotton of the T-shirt. How did Adam know she was with Clay? She hadn't told him where she was going. Hell, she hadn't even known she'd wind up in Paradiso when she'd texted him.

She grabbed the phone from Clay's hand and

hopped off the stool as he swept her beer from the counter and headed for the back rooms.

"Adam? How'd you know I'd be with Clay?"

"C'mon, April. Give me some credit. You're in one big mess. Where else would you go?"

Glancing over her shoulder, she said, "What do you know about my big mess?"

"I know a lot more than you indicated in your text. When you told me the wedding was off and to steer clear of Jimmy, I figured you'd found out."

April gritted her teeth but managed to grind out the question on her lips. "You knew about Jimmy?"

"I did." Adam had the decency to cough. "I'm sorry."

"Why? Why did you…?" April braced her hand against the front door. "Never mind. Don't tell me. I don't want to know."

"April, I know I don't have the right to ask you this, especially after what I just admitted, but do not tell Clay about Jimmy. You haven't told him anything, have you?"

"Not yet." She pounded the door with her fist. It was happening again. "Why shouldn't I tell him?"

"Because if you do, Jimmy will kill me…and then he's gonna kill you."

Chapter Three

"Everything okay?" Clay peered into the living room from the hallway.

April started and spun around, the phone clutched to her chest, her face as white as that wedding dress she'd stripped off. "Yeah."

"Or as okay as things can be with Adam." He cocked his head. "Is he still getting into trouble?"

"You could say that." She held out his phone. "Thanks."

He crossed the room and took the phone from her trembling hand. "Why'd he call for you on my phone? Where's yours?"

"I thought I told you. I took off with nothing— no phone, no money, no ID." She shrugged her stiff shoulders.

"Where'd you get that car?" He jerked his thumb toward the window.

"A—a friend. I got it from a friend."

"What's the story, April?" He held up the beer bottle, the label shredded to bits. "I finished your beer. Do you want another?"

"I'll take one." She smoothed her hands over her face and emerged with her lips stretched into a smile. "There's no real story."

She followed him into the kitchen and sat on the edge of a stool. "I ran out on another wedding. That shouldn't be a surprise to you, of all people."

He popped up from the fridge, beer in hand. He set the new bottle on the counter in front of her. "I never got the whole story on that wedding, either. I guess I can't expect to get the truth out of you when it comes to your wedding to someone else."

"I decided he wasn't the one for me." She pressed the sweating bottle against her pink cheek.

"You just figured that out on the morning of the blessed event?"

She nodded and took a sip of beer.

"What was the hurry? You took off in a borrowed car with nothing? Not even your purse? You didn't have the backbone to tell the poor sap?" He clicked his tongue. "April, April. You're getting worse and worse at ditching weddings and fiancés. At least you had the guts to tell me to my face."

April bit her bottom lip. "H-he's not a good guy, Clay."

"Did he hit you?" His fists curled at his sides, despite his resolve to steer clear of April and her problems.

"No. Nothing like that." She blinked her eyes. "But he has a bad temper, and I didn't want to deal with the fallout. Call me a coward."

"Will he come after you?" Like he never did.

She twisted a lock of blond hair around her finger, and Clay swallowed as he remembered the smell of that hair—all sunshine and foolish dreams.

"He doesn't know where I am. I was actually on my way to Mexico when I saw the highway for Tucson and thought…" She curled her hand around the bottle and took a swig of beer. "Oh, hell. I don't know what I thought. I just had a strong desire to see you again."

"Did you love this guy?" Clay held his breath. He couldn't stand the thought of April in love with someone else, wanting someone else the way she once wanted him.

She rounded her shoulders. "I don't think so."

"You have a bad habit of agreeing to marry men you don't love."

Her blue eyes flashed and her nostrils flared, but she pressed her lips into a thin line.

Had he been fishing? April *had* loved him. Nobody could fake emotion…and passion like that. But something had happened the week before their wedding. It was as if she turned off a switch. When she'd broken the news to him that she was backing out, it hadn't even surprised him.

"Why'd you get engaged…again?" He crossed his arms, digging his fingertips into his biceps. She'd already told him more about why she ended this engagement than why she'd ended their own. Maybe one thing would lead to another.

"I don't know. Maybe I was looking for some

stability. Maybe I was tired of handling everything on my own."

"By everything, you mean Adam." He clenched his jaw. He could've handled Adam. He could've offered stability. He thought that's why she ran. She'd become addicted to drama and what he represented lacked excitement. Hell, he knew he worked too many hours, got too involved in his cases.

"Yes, Adam." Her eyes glittered a dangerous blue as she dragged a fingernail across the label on the bottle.

"Why did he call?"

"To make sure I'd landed here. To make sure I was safe."

Clay snorted. "When has Adam ever been concerned for your safety? Unless he's changed."

"He's had it rough, Clay." She sniffed and swiped the back of her hand across her nose. "He's the one who found Mom."

He passed on the opportunity to remind April that Adam had been a screwup before the murder of their mother. April would defend her brother come hell or high water.

He released a long breath as his stomach rumbled with hunger. "What now? Are you going to Mexico? How are you going to do that without ID?"

"C'mon, Clay." She tilted her head. "I'm a Paradiso girl. I know how to slip across the border with the best of 'em."

He jabbed a finger at the baggy T-shirt she'd picked from his closet. It had never looked so good.

"Are you going to get some clothes? A bag? Toiletries? Or is Adam going to pick up your stuff for you?"

"Oh, no. He can't…he's not going to do that." She flipped her hair over her shoulder. "I don't want him to."

"You mean he couldn't be bothered." He held up his hand as she started her defense of her brother. "Save it. Do you have a friend who can get your stuff? Send it to you? Where is your stuff?"

"Albuquerque. Don't worry about it. It's just that—stuff. Anything I have of importance is right here in Paradiso."

Too bad she didn't mean him. "Your place looks good. Your cousin's taking good care of the house."

She twisted her mouth. "I suppose I should stay with Cousin Meg while I regroup here."

As he carefully picked up her empty bottle and turned toward the trash, he said, "Regroup in Paradiso?"

"I think I should at least try to get my wallet, ID, credit cards and all those other items that tie you to civilization." She clicked her nails against the tile counter. "People do disappear, though, don't they?"

"Your father did it. You thinking of following in his footsteps?"

She dropped her hands in her lap and slumped. "No."

Clay bit the inside of his cheek. Talking to April had become a minefield. He couldn't mention her brother, her mother, her father or her most recent fiancé.

He poked the paper bag containing his burrito, which must be a soggy mess by now. "Are you going to drive to the house? You can call Meg on my phone first to warn her."

She slid from the stool and stretched her arms to the ceiling, the loose T-shirt taking shape around her body. "Can I buy one more day at your place before facing the inquisition over there? I'll even drive into town and pick up some dinner for you. I can hear your stomach growling from over here."

"I'm good." He rubbed his empty belly. "I have some leftover pasta from last night. Do you want some?"

She covered her mouth. "Ugh, no. I can't get the squishing sound of that head hitting the porch out of my head. Makes me feel queasy every time I think about it."

"Do you mind if I eat in front of you?" He plucked up the bag from Rosita's with his fingertips. "This has been through the ringer tonight. Dropped on the ground, probably stepped on and who knows what got into the bag."

"I don't want to think about that, either." She crossed her hands over her chest. "Water?"

Clay retrieved the leftover pasta and a bottle of water from the fridge. He stuck the plastic bowl with the pasta in the microwave and poured the water into a glass with ice. As he placed it in front of April, he said, "You're serious about staying here tonight?"

"If you're serious about having me."

"I don't think I answered either way." The microwave buzzed, and he pivoted away from April as her lips parted. He picked up the bowl and dropped it on the counter as it burned his fingers.

She wrinkled her nose at the steam that rose from the pasta. "Better let me know one way or the other because I'll have to drive to the house, and I'd rather do it before it gets too late."

"Are you worried about who and what's out there?" He took the seat beside her and pointed his fork at the windows in the living room.

"Why did someone leave that head on your porch?" She pinned her hands between her knees, which bounced up and down. "You just found the woman's body today?"

"We found her this afternoon after an image came through from our drone we have out there. She was on our side of the border at the mouth of a tunnel. Nash crawled through the tunnel to see if she left anything behind."

"Like her head?"

"Drugs, money, cell phone." He twirled his fork in the pasta drenched with marinara. "Nothing. They left her with nothing."

"Except the carving of a fly in her cold, dead hand." April jumped off the stool and took a turn around the room. "You didn't answer me."

"Sure, you can stay here for the night." Clay

stuffed a forkful of spaghetti in his mouth. He could resist this woman for one night, couldn't he?

"Thanks, but that's not what I was talking about." She gathered the hem of the T-shirt in her hands, bunching it in her fists. "Why you? Why was that woman's head on your porch?"

He swiped a paper towel across his mouth. "I'm Border Patrol. I found the body. The other agent on the scene is a new guy and doesn't live in town, and Nash's property is too big and those pecan groves are monitored. I'm the default guy."

"It's dangerous that the drug dealers know you and know where you live."

"The cartel members from Mexico don't, neither do the runners coming through. It's just the guys who distribute locally. They're not going to make a move against the agents. That would be suicide for them." He planted his elbows on the counter. "I'm glad you didn't surprise them in the act. You didn't see anyone driving around when you arrived?"

"No, but I wasn't paying attention. I probably passed a couple of cars on the road before the turn-off to your place." She wagged a finger at him. "And before you ask, no, I didn't notice anything about the cars—make, model, color, license plate—nothing. I didn't realize we'd be finding a head on your porch. I would've told that detective if I'd noticed anything."

"What was it about Detective Espinoza that set you off? The man was just doing his job." Clay pushed away the bowl of pasta, losing his appetite all over again.

"Why was he asking about my dress?"

"You're kidding, right?"

"The dress had nothing to do with the head in the box."

"He's a detective. He's supposed to be curious." Clay rubbed his knuckles against the stubble on his jaw. He must look like hell and for once he cared. "What surprised me is that Nash *didn't* ask about the dress."

"Didn't surprise me a bit. That's Nash." A giggle escaped from her lips, and she clapped a hand over her mouth, her blue eyes wide and glassy above her fingers.

"Humor is allowed—even with a head on your porch, *especially* with a head on your porch. It's a coping device."

"Yeah, you're talking to the queen of coping devices." She tapped a fist over her heart.

"Your coping device is to take care of everyone around you and ignore your own pain." Except when she'd left him. He'd always told her to look out for herself, but he didn't think she'd take his advice at the expense of his happiness.

Be careful what you wish for, Archer.

She dipped her head and toyed with the ties at the waistband of his sweats, her hair creating a blond veil around her face. "I've kept you away from your routine tonight."

He glanced down at his dirt-smudged shirt and

dusty boots. He *did* look like hell. "I think that pink box on my porch disrupted my routine...such as it is. But I'll take the hint and hit the shower."

Her head shot up. "I didn't mean that."

"I usually do take a shower as soon as I get off work, especially after a day like today." He snatched the bowl from the counter. "I won't be long. Help yourself to anything in the fridge, or if you're tired, I can make up the bed in the guest room."

"I can do that myself. Sheets?"

"There's bedding in the hall closet, top shelf. I just have a bedspread on that bed, but the sheets in the closet are clean."

Flicking her fingers in the air, she said, "You go ahead. I'll fix the bed."

Clay pushed open the door to his bedroom and tripped to a stop at the discarded dress on the floor. He gathered it in his arms, burying his face in the silky material to inhale the scent of April's perfume, mixed with her own undeniable smell of sweet and spice.

She'd had enough time to spritz on some perfume before the wedding. What really happened? He had a hard time believing April would put up with someone abusive, but she'd been through a lot in her life.

He tucked a trailing bit of lace into the pile in his arm and stepped out of the room. He'd probably never know the truth, just like he'd never know the real reason why she ran out on him.

When he tapped open the door to the guest room

with his toe, April gasped and dropped the stack of folded sheets in her arms on the bed. Still jumpy.

"Sorry. I'm just going to leave this with you." He dumped the dress on a chair in the corner where it flowed over the sides. "You can figure out how you're going to get the sample to Detective Espinoza."

"I will." She nodded. "Pillows?"

"Not sure if I have extras. I'll check."

"Take your shower. I'll look in the closet."

He retreated to his bedroom, snapping the door shut. He peeled off his uniform and dropped it in the hamper in the bathroom.

The warm spray of the shower hit him midchest as he stepped under the water. Bracing his hands against the tile, he dropped his head. What was he doing? Inviting April Hart to stay at his place even one night meant trouble.

He'd never been able to get her out of his mind, out of his heart.

He scrubbed the grit and dust from his hair, digging into his scalp. Now, he'd have to not forget about her all over again.

He finished his shower and pulled on some gym shorts and a T-shirt. With any luck, April would be worn out from her drive and the terror of finding that head, and be fast asleep in his guest room.

He stepped out of the bedroom and peered around the corner at April, camped out on his couch cradling a hot drink, her feet on top of his coffee table. He pulled his bottom lip between his teeth. Luck had it in for him tonight.

"Did you find everything you needed for the bed?"

"All made up, except for the pillows. You don't have any extra, but that's okay. I'll do without." She tapped her feet together. "I made some tea. Hope you don't mind." Her gaze met his above the rim of her cup. "I didn't know you were a tea drinker."

"Those are left over from my mom's visit."

"How's she doing?" April's tight smile made it clear she didn't care how his mom was doing.

Mom had made it clear how she felt about April ditching her only son, practically at the altar.

"She's fine." His gaze darted to her bare feet propped up on his furniture and back to her face. "What time are you leaving tomorrow?"

She slid her feet from the table, curled one leg beneath her and then changed her mind, planting both of them on the floor. "In a hurry to get rid of me? Not that I blame you."

"Not at all." He waved his arms around the room in a grand gesture. "Stay as long as you want."

Her eyes widened for a second. "Be careful."

Pulling back his shoulders, he crossed his arms. He had to get a grip. One side of his mouth curled into a sneer. "Don't worry. Where you're concerned, I'm gonna be careful."

"Good call, Archer." She stretched her arms over her head and faked a yawn. "This show is boring, and I'm beat from that drive."

"I—I just asked about tomorrow because I have work in the morning."

"Whether you're here or not, I can make my way to my own house."

"Okay, I'll leave it to you. Help yourself to breakfast in the morning." His shoulders dropped as he walked to the kitchen to get some water. He'd go to work tomorrow, and she'd be gone by the time he returned—out of his life once again.

He walked into the living room clutching a glass of water and eyeing April, still ensconced on his couch. "Did you leave anything in the car that you need?"

"No, or just some cash in the cup holder."

"Not a great idea. Leaving things in plain sight in your car is what lures thieves to break in."

She tipped her head back against the couch cushion. "Hard to move. Must be the beer, or the six-hour drive."

"I'll get it for you." He pointed at the table to the side of the front door. "Keys to the car?"

"The only keys I have."

"Who does that?" He shook his head as he stalked toward the door and snatched the keys from the table.

Someone who ran out on two weddings, that's who.

He crossed the porch, the warm night air enveloping him as he trooped down the driveway, gravel and dirt crunching beneath each slap of his flip-flops. He pressed the remote, surprised this old beater even had one.

He yanked the door handle, and the dome light flickered. That would have to be replaced soon, but the car belonged to her friend, didn't it?

He shoved his hand in the cup holder, pinching the bills between his fingertips as he pulled them out. His fingers scrabbled in the bottom of the cup holder for any change, tracing the edge of a smooth disc. He grabbed it and pulled it out, cupping it in his palm.

He held his hand beneath the dome light, and his blood froze in his veins.

What the hell was April doing with a calling card from Las Moscas?

Chapter Four

April pushed up from the couch. Clay was sure taking his sweet time out there. He obviously wanted her to leave and probably wanted her in bed before he even came back into the house—just not his bed.

But the way he looked at her with that fire in his hazel eyes gave her the same old thrill. He couldn't hide his attraction to her because he hadn't been schooled in the art of deception, as she had. It had served her well. She probably could've even faked things with Jimmy after what she'd discovered about him—but she hadn't wanted to try.

Adam possessed the same skills as she did—learned from the same master. Adam had never given one hint that he knew what Jimmy did for a living. He'd introduced her to Jimmy and built him up to be this great guy…and she'd allowed Jimmy to sweep her off her feet at just the right time in her life.

Clay burst through the front door, his jaw tight, his face suffused with red rage.

April jerked back, digging her fingernails into the cushions of the couch. "What's wrong?"

"This." He thrust out his hand, and uncurled his fingers. "Why the hell is this in your car?"

She sagged against the couch. The token—she'd left the token with the fly carved onto it in the cup holder. So, it wasn't a coincidence that the headless woman had something similar clutched in her hand.

"I found it."

Clay blinked, and his solid chest heaved. "You found it here? In my driveway?"

That would make the most sense to him. It would get her out of this particular predicament. She found it in his driveway when she drove up and dropped it in the cup holder, not thinking anything about it.

That would wipe the angry look from his face and allow her to squirm away from the truth. Sometimes a girl got tired of squirming.

She folded her hands across her midsection. "No, I didn't find it in your driveway."

"In town, then? On the street?" He spit out possibilities for her, his body stiff and coiled.

"I found it in my ex-fiancé's office."

The color flooded Clay's face again, and he squeezed his fist around the wooden disc. "You know what it is, don't you?"

"It's the calling card of Las Moscas."

"What does it mean, April? Who's your ex-fiancé? What have you gotten yourself into?"

She held up three unsteady fingers. "That's three questions."

"And you're going to answer all three of them."
He strode past her so fast the ends of her hair stirred.

Clay dumped the token on the countertop where
it clattered with a jarring, accusatory tone. "Start
talking. Start telling the truth…for once."

"I didn't know about Jimmy's involvement with
Las Moscas until today. I didn't even know about
Las Moscas until you told me about the cartel." She
hugged herself and sniffed.

"Jimmy what? What's his last name?"

"Verdugo, Jimmy Verdugo."

"You met him in Albuquerque?"

"Yes, when I went to visit Adam."

"Visit from where?"

She lodged the tip of her tongue in the corner of
her mouth. It seemed as if Clay planned to use his
interrogation to get to the bottom of a few other
truths. "I was living in LA."

"That's where you went after…you left me?"

"I got a job in accounting. Lots of accounting
jobs there."

"You hate accounting."

"Had to work."

He ran a hand across his face as if to readjust
his questioning. "Let me guess. Adam knew what
Jimmy was. He probably introduced you."

"I just found that out today, too. Adam knew
Jimmy was a drug dealer, and he did introduce us."
Her nose stung at the betrayal from her brother and
she rubbed the tip.

"That son of a…" Clay slammed his hand against

the counter and the disc skittered across the tile. "How did you find out?"

"Jimmy was busy this morning, before the wedding. Trying to close out some business for his—" she curled her fingers for air quotes "—import/ export business. I took the opportunity to sneak into his office."

"You had to sneak into your fiancé's office?" He rubbed his palm on the thigh of his shorts.

"I know, right?" She pushed her hair from her face. "I had my suspicions about his business before today, but I thought maybe he was engaging in some shady practices. He never wanted me looking at his accounts, even though I'd offered my services for free."

"You're telling me you snuck into his office, saw his books and figured out he was running drugs?"

"You of all people know how these guys operate. Obviously not. While I was snooping in his office, I heard him coming down the hallway with his best man and business associate." She lifted her shoulders. "I hid."

"In that wedding dress?" He jerked his thumb over his shoulder toward the spare room.

"The sliding door to his balcony was open. I stepped outside. If he had pulled those blinds open, I would've been finished." She clenched her teeth against the chill snaking up her spine as she relived that moment of terror.

"You overheard his conversation with his associate?"

She dipped her chin to her chest once. "I did, and I got an earful. Did your mother ever tell you not to eavesdrop because you'd never hear anything good about yourself? Yeah, I'm sure *your* mother told you that."

"What did you hear?" Clay's hazel eyes darkened to deep green, making her pulse flutter.

"It—it's kind of unbelievable." She sank to the couch. "I still have a hard time believing I heard it."

"I'm all ears." He pulled the stool beneath him and straddled it.

"They talked about a drug deal, a shipment from Mexico, but it sounded like they were going to intercept it or something. From their conversation, there was no doubt in my mind that they planned to hijack this shipment for their own. Is that something Las Moscas would do?"

Clay scratched his chin. "No. That's something another organization would do to Las Moscas."

"He definitely had the calling card of Las Moscas in his desk. I stole that before I left."

"Maybe Jimmy's a member of the cartel, and he and his best man are planning a big double-cross."

She put a hand to her throat. "That doesn't sound like it's going to end well for Jimmy and Gilbert."

"Do you care?" He wedged his hands on his knees and hunched forward.

"About Jimmy? No." She drew her knees up to her chest, digging her heels into the cushion of the couch—and Clay didn't even object. "He was using me, Clay. The courtship, the engagement, the wedding—all a big farce. Jimmy never cared about me. He set me up, or Adam set me up."

"Set you up for what?" Clay cocked his head to one side. "What do you have to offer Jimmy Verdugo, a drug dealer? You didn't win the lottery after you left me, did you?"

She swallowed. Every time he said that she left him, the knife twisted deeper into her gut.

"Not money. Connections."

His eyebrows shot up to a lock of dark hair curling on his forehead. "What connections? Your drug-addled brother? Did he think Adam could provide him with a steady stream of clients?"

"Not my brother. My father."

"Your father?" The crease between his eyes deepened. "What the hell does your father have to do with any of this? He disappeared ten years ago after he murdered your mother."

She wrapped her arms around her legs and touched her forehead to her knees. "The authorities never proved he killed her."

"I'm not going down that road with you again, April. What did Jimmy Verdugo want with your father?"

"You know how everyone said my father went to Mexico when he vanished?"

"Yeah, which is why most people around here believe he's guilty."

She balanced her chin on her knees. "Well, Jimmy and Gilbert believe he's some big-time drug lord down there."

"What?" Clay hopped from the stool and sat on the edge of the coffee table in front of her. "That's crazy."

"They mentioned a name, a nickname. You must know it. El Gringo Viejo."

The color ebbed from Clay's tawny complexion. "Jimmy thinks your father, C. J. Hart, is El Gringo Viejo?"

"So, you *do* know him."

"Every Border Patrol and every DEA agent knows of El Gringo Viejo."

"Given what you know about him, could he be my father?"

Clay raised his eyes to the ceiling as if running through facts and dates. "As far as we know, El Gringo Viejo started operating about eight years ago."

"That fits my father's timeline. He'd have been down there eight years ago."

"He moves around a lot. His people are loyal."

"Is he part of Las Moscas? From what Jimmy and Gilbert said, it didn't sound like it."

"He's not part of a cartel. He provides high-quality product to everyone, and lets them figure it out among themselves. He's a freelancer."

"Jimmy was convinced enough to date me and marry me."

"That Jimmy must've been some kind of smooth operator." A muscle flickered at the corner of Clay's mouth, and April wanted to press her lips against it.

She'd settled for Jimmy because he'd been a Clay

clone. Adam didn't admit it on the phone, but he most likely trained Jimmy to push all of her buttons. She'd never love anyone the way she'd loved Clay—still loved him.

"I'm pretty sure right now that Adam coached Jimmy into my heart." She laced her fingers together, and her knuckles blanched.

"I'm sorry." Clay covered her hands with one of his own. "Adam needs an ass-kicking. He must believe this garbage about your father."

"We didn't have a chance to talk about it, but I'm sure he does. He may have even been the one to convince Jimmy of it."

"Why didn't you tell me any of this when you showed up here? Especially when I told you about the carving of the fly?"

"I was getting ready to tell you—most of it, anyway, even though it made me look like a fool."

"Join the club."

Her eye twitched. "But then Adam called."

"What did he say?"

"He told me if I told anyone about Jimmy and his business, Jimmy would kill Adam…and me."

Clay reached forward and wrapped his fingers around her ankle just below the elastic of the green sweats. "Did this guy ever threaten you before?"

"Never."

"But he raised your suspicions somehow. That's why you had to sneak into his office and eavesdrop on him."

"It was just the finances. He was always so vague

about his business. Being an accountant—which you're right, I hate—I was curious about his numbers. He brought in a lot of money, lived a lavish lifestyle."

"Is that how he seduced you?" His fingers tightened around her ankle briefly before he released her.

"Are you calling me a gold digger?" She narrowed her eyes and curled her toes into the cushion of the couch.

"I don't blame you for wanting someone to take care of you. What Jimmy offered must've been attractive after what you've been through."

"I admit, the money made his life seem easy—people to handle the pesky details, private trainers, personal chefs, private jet. I was living in some kind of fairy tale until I woke up in that office and realized how fake everything was—including my feelings for Jimmy."

"I'm assuming Jimmy knows you ditched the wedding because you found out about him and his motives. Can Adam spin it? You got cold feet? Hell, it *is* kind of a pattern for you." Clay smacked his palm against his chest. "In fact, this is what I recommend you do. Call Jimmy and apologize for running out. Tell him you're not ready. Tell him you went back to your ex."

April's heart skipped a beat. *If only.*

"How long did you know him before the wedding?"

"Six months." She pulled her hair back from her face. "This could work."

"Perfect. You were too hasty." Clay pushed off the table and stepped over it on his way to the kitchen. "Do you think that moron brother of yours kept his mouth shut about you? He needs to convince Jimmy you don't know anything about his dirty business."

"I don't think he told Jimmy I eavesdropped on the conversation with Gilbert." She twisted her fingers. "I did take that carving, though. He probably missed it."

"Where was it?"

"It was one of several in his desk."

"Maybe he won't miss it. What would it mean to you, anyway?" Clay turned around, his phone in his hand. "You didn't tell Jimmy I was Border Patrol, did you?"

"I didn't tell Jimmy anything about you, other than I had been engaged before and ended things right before the wedding." April folded her hands and pinned them between her knees. She hadn't wanted to tell Jimmy anything about Clay—never even told him his name.

"That's good." He held up the phone. "Do you think it's too late to call Adam and warn him to stay quiet?"

"I can't believe Adam even kept your number in his phone."

"Probably insurance. Figured I could get him out of a jam if he ever needed the help."

"That sounds about right." She snapped her fingers. "I'll call Adam and find out. And if he told Jimmy that I know he's a drug dealer?"

"You'll have to convince Jimmy you won't tell anyone."

Clay placed the phone in her outstretched hand, and she went to his recent calls and tapped Adam's number. At the first ring, she leaned forward. At the second, she glanced at Clay. Adam's cell rang for a third time, and April licked her lips.

When the phone tripped over to Adam's voice mail, she put Clay's phone on speaker. "What now?"

"Don't leave a message." Clay lunged for the phone and ended the call. "Just in case."

"Just in case—" April pressed her fingers against her throbbing temple "—Jimmy has Adam's phone?"

"Or he gets to his voice mail. You don't want anything on record."

"Should I call Jimmy now?"

"Not from my phone." He held up his cell and then returned it to its charger on the counter. "You can pick up a burner phone tomorrow and call him from that. Maybe Adam will see the missed call from me and get back to you."

"I wonder why he didn't pick up." April rubbed her arms. "It's a little early for him to be in bed."

"Maybe he's with Jimmy and doesn't want to answer any calls, which would be the smart move." Clay lifted an eyebrow. "Is Adam still using?"

"Says he's not." She hunched her shoulders.

"But you don't believe him."

"You may think I'm overly protective where Adam is concerned, but that doesn't mean I don't see him for what he is."

"He's your brother. I understand." Clay grabbed his water glass and set it in the sink. "You can stay here if you want to watch TV. The spare room doesn't have one. I'm going to hit the sack. Unlike Adam, it's not too early for me, especially after the day I had."

"You must be exhausted." She pointed the remote at the TV screen where she'd paused her movie. "I guess I'll stay here and try to unwind a little."

"I'll toss one of my pillows onto your bed." He lifted his hand and disappeared into the hallway.

April let out a long breath she hadn't even realized she'd been holding. Being in the same room as Clay hadn't been as easy as she'd expected—even after coming clean about Jimmy.

Could she really call Jimmy tomorrow and act normal? Act as if she didn't know he was a drug-dealing scumbag who wanted to marry her to get to her father?

She restarted the movie and adjusted a throw pillow behind her neck. Sure she could. She'd been lying to Clay Archer for years.

Chapter Five

Clay woke with a start, his heart thrumming in his chest. *April.* She'd come back into his life, dragging her drama along with her.

He threw back the covers, fully awake, and planted his bare feet on the cool tile floor. His clock radio sounded the alarm with the news at six and he reached over and smacked it off.

He crept from his room and grabbed the door-jamb when he saw the door to the spare room ajar. The hinges creaked as he pushed it open.

Clay's jaw tightened as he scanned the neatly made-up bed. At least she hadn't left a mess when she sneaked out of here.

Grabbing the back of his neck, he dug his fingers into his knotted muscles. He'd told her what to do to alleviate Jimmy's suspicions. It was up to her to follow through.

He padded on bare feet into the darkened living room and flicked on the light in the kitchen. As he measured ground coffee in the filter, a soft moan floated on the air and he dropped the filter on the counter.

He charged into the living room, his fists clenched at his sides. A lump on the couch elongated, and a swath of blond hair rippled over the edge of the cushion.

He crept closer and peered down at April's face, smooth in sleep except for a tiny crease between her eyebrows. She never could sleep soundly. What sinister dreams clouded her mind, creating that little line?

Her lips parted and she emitted a sigh that stirred the strands of shiny hair crisscrossing her cheek.

His fingers twitched to smooth the hair away from her face, but he didn't want to disturb her sleep. God knows, she needed it. What had possessed her to marry a man she hardly knew? Stability? He could've offered her that and more. Protection for Adam? That he'd never offer.

He turned away from her, cleaned up the coffee mess in the kitchen, set up another cup to brew and retreated to his bedroom. For those few minutes, he'd almost come to terms with having April out of his life again.

He took a quick shower and dressed in his uniform. Maybe they'd find out the identity of the dead drug mule today. If she had fingerprints on file somewhere, they'd ID her soon enough. It would take longer to match the DNA from the head to the body, but how many bodies without heads could there be in one day?

He pulled on his boots and returned to the kitchen where his coffee awaited him, the smell of the rich brew giving him a jolt. As he screwed on the lid to his commuter mug, April coughed from the other room.

She called out, "Are you still here?"

"Sorry if I woke you up." He'd had just the lights beneath the counters on, and he turned on the overhead lights. "Do you want some coffee? I have just a single-brew machine, but I can put some on for you now."

She sat up and yawned. "I think I'll have more of your mother's tea, if that's okay. I know your mom would probably mind, but she's not here."

"Did you sleep okay? Why didn't you use the bedroom? You don't even have a blanket or pillow out here."

She shrugged the afghan from her shoulders. "I found this on the chair. I fell asleep in front of the TV and just got too comfortable to move."

"I've spent a few nights on that couch in front of the TV myself." He put down his coffee mug and grabbed a tea bag from the shelf. "I'll leave the tea for you here, and you're welcome to cook breakfast before you head out to Meg's."

"Maybe I'll drive up to Tucson today and get some clothes…and that phone." She tousled her hair. "I suppose I have to make that call to Jimmy."

"I think that's your safest bet right now. How are your acting skills?"

She jerked up her head. "Pretty darned good."

"Then you shouldn't have any trouble convincing Jimmy you made a mistake, you're sorry, it's you not him. Blah, blah. You've done it before."

Clay snapped his mouth shut and sealed his lips. Reminding April what she'd done was not going to persuade her to open up to him and tell him the real reason why she left. He needed to give it a rest.

He buckled his equipment belt around his waist and holstered his gun. Grabbing his hat, he turned at the door. "When you get that phone, give me a call. I left my number on a sticky note that I slapped on a cabinet door."

He paused on the threshold. "Don't hang around here too long, April. There are some bad characters who know where I live. I'll have the Paradiso PD cruise by here a few times in the next hour."

"You just creeped me out." She pushed up from the couch. "I can shower at Meg's and get breakfast there, too."

"Do you want me to wait until you're ready to go?" He glanced at the phone clutched in his hand. "I'm not going to be late, and I'm leaving early to pick up Denali."

"Is he okay?"

"He's fine." He tapped his cheekbone. "Just a minor eye irritation and I would've picked him up yesterday, but I got called out on that dead body. Drew offered to take him home for the night."

"Small-town vets." Her gaze shifted to the great outdoors behind him. "If you don't mind waiting, I'll hurry."

"Take your time." He patted the case slung over his shoulder. "I can check emails on my laptop."

By the time he'd powered up his computer and clicked on the first email, April had returned, the bedraggled wedding dress thrown over her shoulder like the pelt of some wild animal.

"That was fast. No shower?"

"Told you, I'll take one at the house." She plucked at the baggy sweats that couldn't conceal her shapely backside. "I didn't have anything to change into, anyway. I'll borrow some clothes from Meg."

"Do you want me to take this to the station for you?" He tugged on the hem of the wedding dress. "It's on my way."

"Could you?" She sloughed the dress from her shoulder as if shedding a layer of skin.

The dress landed in a heap between them. "That would really help me out because I wouldn't have to explain anything to Meg about the wedding."

"My lips are sealed, but plenty of people saw you last night all decked out in your finest bridal attire." He left the dress on the floor and shut down his laptop. "You know how this town likes gossip."

"I know more than anyone." She brushed off the front of her T-shirt. "I'll deal with it when it happens. One thing at a time."

"You got it." He stuffed his computer in his bag and hitched it over his shoulder. Then he gathered the dress in his arms, resting his chin on the yards of fabric. Probably the closest he'd ever get to a wedding dress.

Tipping his head toward the door, he said, "Lead the way."

April scurried in front of him and held the door open as he squeezed past her. She grabbed the keys jingling from his outstretched hand and hit the remote for his truck.

"No ceremony needed. Just stuff it in the back seat." She opened the back door of his truck.

He shoved it inside, punching and squishing it into submission. It frothed over the headrest of the front seat. He yanked it down. "This thing is alive."

"Yeah, not really my taste. I'm just gonna claim temporary insanity."

He eyed her car over her shoulder. "You sure that thing runs?"

"It got me here, didn't it? I'll be fine." She tossed his key chain at him. "Thanks for sticking around."

"How long will you be in Paradiso?"

"Long enough to regroup and think about my next move."

"You're not really considering trying to track down your father in Mexico, are you?"

"I don't know. What if he really is El Gringo Viejo?"

"And your knowing that and tracking him down in Mexico would benefit you, how?" His hand shot out, and he encircled her wrist with his fingers. "Let that go, April. Let it all go. Call Jimmy and let him know the engagement was a mistake and you're out of his life, and then get back to *your* life."

Her lashes swept over her eyes. "I just might do that."

She wobbled across his gravel driveway, a pair of pearly white pumps sticking out of the bottom of the sweats.

Shaking his head, he climbed into his truck. The wedding gown tickled the back of his neck, so he slapped at it and cranked on his engine. The truck idled behind April's car.

When her brake and reverse lights flashed, Clay backed out and rolled backward down the road to allow April to pull out ahead of him. He followed her to the fork, and she stuck her hand out the window as she peeled out, making a left turn.

He took a right and aimed the truck back toward town. Detective Espinoza worked for the county sheriff's department but he'd be camped out at the Paradiso PD station for the next week at least, to get a handle on this investigation.

When Clay reached the police department, he pulled into the small parking lot on the side for official vehicles. He swung open the back door and scowled at the dress. He should've offered April a pair of scissors to cut out the bloodstained material.

He wrestled the dress out of the car, and a male voice called out over the parking lot. "Is that your new girlfriend, Archer?"

Clay lifted his hand and flashed a one-finger salute at the cop and then gathered the dress to his chest, wrapping his arms around the voluminous material.

Ten of the dress April had planned to wear to their own wedding could fit inside this one flouncy mess. He'd seen the dress when he'd gone over to her house to pick up a few of his things when she left town. The picture in his mind of her in it had stayed with him longer than he cared to admit.

He staggered to the building, tripping on the dress more than once. He pushed into the lobby of the PD and peered around his delivery at Todd Barton, the officer at the front desk, wide-eyed and mouth gaping.

"This is for Espinoza. It has the blood from the head last night."

"Oh, right." Barton jumped from his chair and came out from behind the counter. "I'll take it into one of the rooms in the back and cut out the swaths of material we need and bag them for testing. Espinoza has already sent blood samples from the, uh… head to the state."

"She's all yours." Clay pressed the wedding dress against Barton's chest and brushed his hands together as if ridding himself of a dirty task.

Barton poked his head to the side of the white suds. "Are you going to take this back with you after I cut out the samples?"

"No way." Clay turned on his heel, almost bumping into Espinoza as he charged through the door.

"Just the man I'm looking for."

"I just dropped off the dress with the bloodstains

from the severed head." Clay jerked his thumb over his shoulder at Barton, as if there was more than one blood-smeared wedding dress.

"Archer, we've got a problem." Espinoza rubbed the back of his neck.

Clay's pulse jumped. "What kind of problem?"

"That body you found yesterday and that head on your porch—they don't match."

APRIL CUPPED THE cell phone in her sweaty palm and dumped it on the table. She waved to the waitress balancing three plates in her hand. Once she delivered the food, the waitress scurried to her table.

"More iced tea?"

"Actually, I'm looking for an outlet." April dangled the charging cord from her fingers. "Just bought a new phone, and I need to charge it up."

"We can do that for you behind the counter." The server held out her hand, wiggling her fingers, and April pressed the phone and the charger into her palm.

"Thanks, and I'll have more iced tea when you get a chance."

The waitress smiled, but her eyes assessed April—hard.

April nodded and ducked her head to slurp some lukewarm tea through the straw. Had this young woman cut her teeth on crazy April Hart stories? Did she recognize her?

Meg had been suspicious of April's story about rushing out to help a friend—not that she expected her cousin to believe anything she said, but that fabrication sounded more worthy than the fact that she'd run out on a wedding—again.

Mom's side of the family always slept with one eye open around her and Adam, as if they'd inherited Dad's killer gene or something. Not that she was totally convinced her father murdered her mother. They'd had their problems and Dad was always a scammer, but he'd also loved Mom—or he'd been an incredible actor…or a sociopath.

If Dad were really this El Gringo Viejo character like Adam thought, maybe he did kill Mom because she found out something. Like *she'd* found out about Jimmy.

"Your phone is charging." The waitress hovered over the table with a plate of food in one hand and a pitcher of iced tea in the other. "And here's your sandwich."

She placed the plate on the table and filled up the iced tea glass. "Do you want a cup of ice for that?"

"Sure, thanks." April whipped her napkin into her lap and picked up one half of her turkey sandwich.

The front door of the café swung open and April nearly choked on her first bite as Clay charged through the door, his dark hair already askew.

"Glad I found you." He held up his hand to the waitress. "Can you bring me a cola, Larissa?"

Clay dragged the chair out across from her, scraping it across the tile floor, and sat down. "You're not gonna believe this."

Still chewing, April pointed to her mouth. She swallowed and took a sip of tea. "You almost made me choke on my food when you barged in here. I don't want a repeat. What is going on?"

Clay gripped the edge of the table as if to brace himself. "That head we found yesterday on my porch?"

"Yeah, I remember it." She nabbed a spot of spicy mustard from the corner of her mouth with the tip of her tongue.

"It does not belong to the headless body at the border."

The room tilted and April twisted the napkin in her lap. "What do you mean? There's another body without a head out there and another head missing its body?"

"Exactly." He rubbed his knuckles across his jaw. "That's crazy, even for Paradiso, even so close to the border."

April pushed away her plate, one perfect bite missing from her sandwich. "I don't understand. How did they discover that so quickly? You told me the DNA would take a while."

"Espinoza doesn't have the DNA test back yet, but the medical examiner has determined that the body belongs to a young Latina and the head is that of an older, Caucasian woman."

Goose bumps raced up and down her arms and she folded them across her chest. "How is this even possible? And why was the older woman's head left on your porch when you found the body of the younger woman?"

"They're obviously connected, from the same hit. Maybe both women came through the tunnel, Las Moscas killed the younger one there, leaving her body and taking her head, and then murdered the other woman elsewhere, dumped her body and left her head for me—just to mess with us."

"It's pure evil, isn't it?" April rubbed her arms. "Do they think this is some kind of joke?"

"This is business, and they're deadly serious." He glanced up at the waitress. "Thanks, Larissa." He sucked down half his soda before coming up for air.

"How'd you track me down here?" She poked at her sandwich. Coming to Paradiso had seriously done a number on her appetite.

"Happened to see your car out front as I was driving through town, and I remember this used to be one of your favorite places. I wasn't sure you'd be back from Tucson yet."

She leaned back and ran her finger around the neck of her new T-shirt. "Picked up some clothes and bought a phone."

"Did you make the call yet?" He picked up the untouched half of her sandwich. "Are you going to eat this, or did I just ruin your appetite?"

"You can have it and my new phone is charging behind the counter, so I haven't called Jimmy yet." She drummed her fingers on the table next to her plate. "What does Espinoza think about the two murders?"

"Same." He waved the sandwich in the air. "It's obvious they're connected."

"Really? 'Cause this morning you thought it was obvious that the head belonged to the body by the border."

"Good point." He scooted the plate back in front of her. "I'm feeling guilty. Eat your lunch."

She picked up the sandwich and nibbled on the crust. "How is Espinoza going to ID the body, fingerprints?"

"That's first, but if she never committed a crime and she's a Mexican national, we may not get a hit. Missing persons, maybe."

The waitress swung by again. "Clay, do you want to order something? I'm off in five."

"I just demolished half of my…friend's sandwich. I'm good, but I'll take a refill on my soda before you leave."

Friends? Is that what they were?

April cleared her throat. "And I'll take my phone and the check."

"Oh, your phone. I'll get that for you."

Larissa spun away, and April wrinkled her nose. "She looks familiar. The name is familiar, too."

"Her family has lived here for some time. She was into the drug scene for a while, but I think she's clean now."

April hunched forward. "Then she probably knows who I am?"

"That you're my ex-fiancée or that you're the daughter of C. J. Hart?"

"Both. Either."

He shrugged, a quick lift and drop of his shoulders. "Don't be paranoid, April."

"If you say so."

"How'd it go with Meg?"

"All right, except she kept watching me as if she expected me to steal the silver—and she doesn't even have any silver."

"There you go again." He nudged her small purse at the edge of the table. "She must've fronted you a little money to get you back on your feet."

"She did, but she is living in my house rent free."

"You're letting her live there without paying you anything? That's generous of you. There's a little housing shortage in Paradiso due to the new pecan-processing plant. You could get some bucks for that house."

"I don't know." She dragged her new purse in front of her and unzipped it. "I feel like I kind of owe it to her."

"You're not responsible for what your father did."

"Or didn't do."

His mouth tightened. "You don't owe your mother's family anything, April, no matter how guilty they make you feel."

Larissa set another glass in front of Clay. "Your drink, and your phone."

"Thanks." April studied the woman's dark brown eyes and shy smile. Then she snapped her fingers. "I know you. You dated my brother, Adam Hart, for a while, didn't you?"

Larissa's eyes widened. "Yeah, I did. I didn't think you'd remember me, but I remembered you."

"Well, it's good to see you again." April scooped up the phone and waited while Larissa put down the check and left the table. "Maybe I should try calling Adam again, too."

"First things first. Give Jimmy a call and clear the air." Clay half rose from his chair. "I'll give you some privacy."

"I don't need privacy to talk to Jimmy." She waved him back to his seat and tapped Jimmy's number into the phone.

She held her breath through the first ring and second ring, hoping for a voice mail.

"Who's this?"

Jimmy's voice, abrupt and gravelly, made her jump. He'd put on a totally different act when they'd met, but he couldn't keep it up forever, and even before she overheard his conversation with Gilbert, doubts had crept into her mind.

"Jimmy, this is April. I—I just wanted to explain what happened and to apologize."

"Are you coming back home, April?" His voice softened and a pleading tone had crept into it.

She lined up her spine against the back of her chair. "No. No, I'm not coming back, Jimmy."

"Then you'd better return what you stole, bitch, or I'm comin' for you."

Chapter Six

April clutched the phone so hard its edges dug into her palm. "The ring? You want the ring back?"

"I'm not talking about the ring—cubic zirconium, anyway."

Jimmy chuckled, which caused her fear to spike even more. Had he missed that wooden token?

"I don't know what you're talking about, Jimmy. The dress? The wedding. I'll pay you back for all of it."

Clay had shifted in his seat and curled his hands into fists where they rested on the table.

"Don't play with me, April. You took the flash drive from my laptop—and I want it back."

She let out a slow breath. She didn't take any flash drive, didn't even see one in the laptop on the desk. "I didn't take your flash drive. Why would I do that?"

Clay cocked his head, and she shrugged.

Jimmy paused. "You were in my office yesterday morning before you took off. I know you were. I found some beads or whatever from the wedding gown. So, you must've been dressed for the wedding and decided to snoop on me. Why?"

April swallowed. This had to be a good turn of events. He didn't seem sure that she knew about his business—and she wanted to keep it that way.

"I went into your office looking for you, to tell you I was having second thoughts. Who knows? If I had found you there, maybe you could've talked me off the ledge, but you weren't there and I left. That's it, Jimmy. I wasn't snooping on you. I didn't take any flash drive."

"Have you talked to Adam?"

"He called me yesterday just to make sure I was okay. We didn't talk long."

"How'd he reach you? I've been trying your phone ever since I realized you'd skipped out. You ditched it or it's not turned on."

"I'd rather not say, Jimmy. It's over and I'll be happy to pay you what I owe you for the wedding— even the cheap ring—but I didn't take anything from you and I'm not coming back. Why is this flash drive so important, anyway, and why would I want to take it?"

Clay kicked her under the table and she wagged a finger at him. She had to keep pretending she had no idea the nature of his business. She'd asked a normal question from an innocent person.

"Important information about my import/export business, and I know you were always asking questions about it."

"Just out of curiosity. I'm sorry someone took

the flash drive but it seems like you're more upset about the missing flash drive than your missing bride, so it appears that I made the right decision. Goodbye, Jimmy."

Before he could answer, she ended the call and closed her eyes, the phone cradled between her hands.

"What the hell was that all about?"

She opened one eye and peered at Clay. "He doesn't know. He thinks I stole some flash drive because he knew I had been in his office, but he seemed to believe me when I told him I hadn't taken it."

"As far as he let on." He traced a bead of moisture on the outside of his glass. "I get that you didn't want to show your hand, but he didn't, either. He may still think you took the flash drive, but didn't want to get into a back-and-forth with you on the phone."

April plucked the straw from her iced tea glass and nibbled on the end. "I wonder what's on the flash drive."

"What did he say? You asked him."

"Business stuff." She tapped the straw against her tooth, flicking droplets of liquid on the table. "I'll bet it's business stuff. I wonder who took it. One of his so-called friends probably."

"You don't think Adam stole it, do you?"

A feather of apprehension brushed the back of her neck. That had crossed her mind as soon as

Jimmy mentioned the theft, but she'd pushed it away as disloyalty.

"Why would Adam steal info about Jimmy's business?"

"C'mon, April. This is Adam we're talking about. If he could get rich quick, he'd do it and damn the torpedoes. What better way than to butt in on someone's drug trade."

Heat flared in her cheeks. "Adam wouldn't…"

She trailed off in the face of Clay's hard stare. He'd never had any patience for her coddling of Adam. He would always take her side over Adam's.

"You know he would, April. Didn't he set you up with Jimmy? Why'd he do that? Why'd he facilitate a relationship between you and a drug dealer?" Clay slammed his fist on the table. "If I ever get my hands on that boy, he's really gonna need the drugs."

Sighing, April buried her chin in the palm of her hand. "You don't understand him."

"I know he found your mom in a pool of blood, stabbed to death." Clay traced his knuckle down her forearm to her elbow planted on the table. "He went through hell, but he didn't have to drag you along with him. You had your own hell to deal with."

"I'm not saying I forgive him for setting me up with Jimmy, but that doesn't mean he stole the flash drive. He'd have to know that Jimmy would think I did it."

"Yeah."

She fished some money from her purse, and

Clay closed his hand around her fingers. "You'd better keep that until you pick up your debit and credit cards or get them replaced." He pulled out his own wallet and tossed some bills on the table. "Any chance that brother of yours can send your stuff to you? ID, cards, clothes?"

"I don't think that's going to happen. As long as Jimmy believes me, I'm safe enough. I can take a drive back up to Albuquerque and collect my stuff myself. I have a debt to pay back up that way, anyway."

"You're not really going to reimburse Jimmy for the wedding, the dress and the cheap ring, are you?"

"No, but I used that cheap ring to buy a car, and now the poor seller is out a car and the cash. I'm sure he got a rude surprise when he tried to hock the ring."

"You told me you borrowed that car from a friend." Clay's lips twisted into a half smile. "What other lies have you told me, April Hart?"

April kept her head down as she stuffed her cash back into the purse in her lap.

You have no idea, Clay Archer.

CLAY LEFT APRIL at her car with assurances from her that she wouldn't head back to New Mexico without him. He had to question his own sanity for getting involved with April again, but he couldn't just abandon her. She'd gotten mixed up with some dangerous folks and even if she were convinced Jimmy Verdugo had let her off the hook, he wasn't.

When he got back to the office, it was still buzzing with the news that the head and body didn't match. He didn't want to think about where that other head was going to turn up. Maybe on another agent's porch. And the other body? It could be anywhere in the desert.

He sat down behind his desk and two minutes later Valdez plopped down in a chair across from him.

"What do you make of it, Archer? There must've been two mules coming across the border."

"Looks like it." Clay kicked his feet up on the corner of his desk. "Two mules who were sent to intercept a shipment designated for Las Moscas. Two sacrifices. Whoever planned this had to know it was a death sentence for the mules."

"Canaries in a coal mine?" Valdez steepled his fingers and gazed over the tips like some kind of drug muse. "They send these two unsuspecting women to do the dirty work to see if they could get away with stealing from Las Moscas. Next time they'll try something else."

"You're probably right, Valdez." Clay dropped his feet to the floor and flipped up the lid of his laptop. "I'm gonna do some work. Did you finish the report from last night yet?"

Valdez reddened to the roots of his hair as he pushed up to his feet. "I did not. I just got the sheriff's report today. Do you want to check it over before I submit it?"

"Your last report was good. I trust you."

When Valdez had tripped off with a smile engulfing the bottom half of his face, Clay began tapping away on his keyboard.

Surely, April had done a cursory search for Jimmy Verdugo. She wouldn't date and then decide to marry some guy without doing a little research first. She didn't have the same resources he did, but she would've been able to search for a criminal record.

The woman had impulsive tendencies, but she had a healthy dose of skepticism. The only way she could've wound up so deep with Jimmy is if Adam engineered the whole thing.

April made the mistake of seeing her brother as a hapless druggie with PTSD. Adam might be a junkie with PTSD, but he was far from hapless. He used April with a cunning that she refused to acknowledge.

Clay had no doubt Adam had fed info to Jimmy about April—her likes, her dislikes, her wants, her needs. But why had April been so willing to marry someone…even if he were the perfect guy?

She'd twisted his heart and wrung it dry so thoroughly he didn't know if he could ever love another again. In fact, here he was, ready to do her bidding, ready to protect her. And in the end, she'd walk away from him.

Clay accessed the NCIC database and entered Jimmy Verdugo's name. He cocked his head at the display. None of these people could be a match for

April's Jimmy. His mouth tightened. No, *not* April's Jimmy.

Even though his search of Jimmy had returned some James Verdugos, he entered James for the criteria this time.

He stared at the same results and sucked in his bottom lip. How did an associate of Las Moscas have a clean criminal record?

Maybe Jimmy hadn't been in this country long enough to have a record here. April hadn't mentioned if he'd been born here or not.

Clay's fingers hovered over the keyboard. He didn't have any probable cause on the guy to request a report from Interpol on any activities in another country.

He shouldn't even be using NCIC for personal lookups, but he could always justify his actions based on the carved fly April had found in Jimmy's office.

Taking a deep breath, he switched to a different database and did a search on El Gringo Viejo. Several releases popped up, but no pictures. Nobody had ever taken a photograph of El Gringo Viejo— at least not that they knew of.

Where had Adam gotten the crazy idea that his father was El Gringo Viejo? Clay squinted at the small print of the reports online. The dates did match up and C. J. Hart probably did cross the border after murdering his wife, but what else did Adam have?

If he could get his hands on April's brother, he'd interrogate him—after he got finished thrashing him.

The ringing of his office phone jarred his thoughts, and he picked it up after the first ring.

"Clay, this is Dr. Drew. Denali is more than ready to come home."

Clay's gaze darted to the time at the bottom corner of his screen. "Sorry, Dr. Drew. I didn't realize how late it was."

"No problem. I have him at the office with me and we'll be here for another few hours."

"I'll leave right now."

Clay hung up the phone and started to pack up his gear for the day. Denali would be overjoyed to see April. That dog loved her and would never forget her.

Clay snorted. Like master like dog.

APRIL SECURED HER purchases in the trunk of the car that really didn't belong to her. Poor Ryan. He'd probably gone to the pawn shop, found out the real worth of the ring and figured she'd double-crossed him.

On the way back to Albuquerque, she'd try to find Ryan and return the car—or buy it from him. Adam had been borrowing her car, and she'd left the fancy wheels Jimmy had bought her parked in his garage. Knowing what she knew now, Jimmy probably never bought her that car. It was either a lease or a purchase in his name.

How could she have been so stupid? She'd been

manipulated by both Adam and Jimmy. This had to be the last straw with her brother. He'd done nothing but take from her, but she'd made it easy for him. She'd given up so much for him and had gotten nothing but betrayal in return.

Once she got back to New Mexico, she could make herself whole again—pick up her identity, literally—and start again.

And Clay? There had been no expiration date on that threat two years ago. Back in Paradiso, someone could be watching her right now.

She glanced over her shoulder as she got into her car.

Meg would still be at work at the pecan-processing plant, thank goodness. April didn't need her cousin's judgment right now—and Meg didn't even know about the ditched wedding.

April pulled up outside the neat, white picket fence surrounding a garden of succulents. The cacti had already shed their spring flowers, but their prickly stoicism always struck an answering chord in her heart. There they stood with their arms raised through the scorching desert heat, the dry winds and even the monsoons that swept through southern Arizona in the fall.

Tears welled in her eyes. This garden had been her mother's pride and joy. Her mother had been a transplant to the arid Sonoran Desert, deficient in rolling green lawns and neat concrete driveways and delicate dewy flowers, so Mom had created her own oasis, drawing from the beauty of the desert.

April sniffed and exited the car. She circled around the back to collect her packages, and then swung through the front gate.

She strode up the brick walkway, her step faltering as she caught sight of a brown box on the porch. She puffed out a breath. Meg told her she ordered a lot of items online to save trips into Tucson.

She wouldn't have even experienced that small frisson of fear that zipped through her veins if Clay hadn't found her in the coffee shop this afternoon and told her about the second body.

She rolled her shoulders back and continued to approach the porch. She took one step up, shook out the house key Meg had given her earlier and nudged the box with her toe. It didn't look like a delivery, as it had no address label.

She kicked the box. It jumped an inch. A trickle of blood seeped from the bottom.

Chapter Seven

Clay punched the accelerator of his truck and it lurched forward from the stop sign, causing Denali to slide off the seat.

"Sorry, boy." Clay patted the passenger seat and Denali scrambled back onto it.

What the hell was going on in this town? Why would someone leave that head on April's porch?

The perpetrators must still be in Paradiso. They'd connected April to him somehow, and decided to double down on their message. What was their message if not a threat?

His foot pressed on the gas pedal and his truck growled in response. Denali panted beside him, their reunion cut short when he got the call from Espinoza about April finding a head in a box on her porch. She must be regretting her visit to Paradiso even more now.

He rolled past her address and kept going, as emergency vehicles clogged the street in front of her house. The scene must remind her of the night

Adam found their mother's body on the kitchen floor, and his heart ached for her all over again.

He parked the truck and slid out. He came around and opened the door for Denali. If he didn't let him out, the dog would be howling and eventually scratch through the door.

Denali kept up with Clay's long stride, undeterred by the lights and activity, nose in the air, ears pricked forward. Did he smell April already?

Clay spotted her talking to Detective Espinoza, her arms folded, her face a pale oval. Denali must've detected her at the same time because he tore away from Clay's side, making a beeline for April.

When she saw the dog running toward her, April dropped to her knees and wrapped her arms around his squirming body, burying her face in his gray-and-white fur.

When she looked up to meet Clay's eyes, tears streaked her face, but a wide smile claimed her lips. "He looks great."

To reward the compliment, Denali licked the tears from April's face.

Clay shifted his gaze to Espinoza. "Is it our girl from the border?"

"Without any scientific proof, I'd say it is. The head belongs to a young Latina. I paid attention this time, but maybe I shouldn't make any assumptions."

Clay swore. "Two heads, one body down, one body to go. What kind of game are they playing and why involve April?"

"They must've seen her with you, although why

Las Moscas is targeting you is puzzling." Espinoza eyed him beneath the brim of his hat as if inspecting a bug.

"Hey, I have no clue." Clay held up his hands. "If you think I've been on their payroll or something, you're welcome to check me out. Do a full investigation. You won't find anything."

"Don't get your back up, but if you can think of any reason why Las Moscas would be more interested in you than any other Border Patrol agent in the area, let me know."

"Maybe because I'm one of the few who lives in Paradiso. What surprises me is that someone is still lurking around depositing body parts in town. Usually, strangers are executing strangers at the border and leaving us to clean up after them."

April popped up beside them, brushing her hands together. "Has anyone notified my cousin yet? She should be home from work soon and she's going to be freaked out by all this. Do you think at least the head will be gone by the time she gets home?"

"April." Clay took her by the shoulders. "You don't need to worry about Meg right now. Are you all right?"

She swiped a hand beneath her red-tipped nose. "It was like déjà vu all over again—only the box wasn't as pretty this time. At least I knew enough not to pick it up, so the head didn't go bounding down the walkway."

The glassy blue of her eyes and the slight quiver

to her bottom lip were the only contradictions to her flip words.

His fingers caressed her flesh beneath the light cotton of the blue T-shirt that matched her eyes. "I'm sorry you had to go through this again. It's my fault they left that for you."

"It's not your fault. It's your job." She addressed Espinoza. "Do you have the right head this time?"

"We think so, but we'll run the tests to make sure." Espinoza pointed down the street. "The Paradiso PD officers canvassed the neighborhood and, just like at your place, Archer, nobody saw a thing."

"If someone did, do you really think they'd step forward?" Clay scratched the top of Denali's head, still shaking with joy at his reunion with April. "People around here are familiar with Las Moscas. They're going to keep their heads down and not interfere with business. They don't want the violence at the border creeping up here."

A wail from the street had Denali stiffening and pointing his head, nostrils quivering a mile a minute.

"Oh, boy. Here comes Meg." April adjusted her position, pulling her shoulders back and widening her stance as if getting ready for a tackle.

Denali got ready, too, leaving Clay's side to take up his position in front of April.

Meg came bobbing and weaving up the walkway as if trying to gain purchase on the deck of a ship, a helpless Paradiso PD officer trailing in her wake, hand outstretched.

"A head? Did I hear that right? A head was on my porch?" Meg, all five feet of her, steamrolled up to Detective Espinoza. "Somebody out there told me a head was on my porch."

Espinoza, his face impassive, asked, "Are you the owner of the house, ma'am?"

"No, but I live here." Meg flung out an arm toward April. "She owns the house."

Meg stopped flapping her lips, froze and then turned toward April. "This is you, isn't it? You come back to Paradiso and heads start appearing on porches wherever you are."

Denali emitted a little growl. He'd never bitten anyone in his life, but he just might make an exception if Meg continued her verbal assault on April.

"Whoa, wait a minute, Meg." Clay took a step between her and April. "This is all me. It has something to do with a body of a mule we found at the border yesterday."

Meg's light-colored eyes flicked in his direction. "You *would* say that."

"It's the truth, Ms.….?" Espinoza's question hung in the air unanswered. "These are two dead women, involved in the drug trade, murdered by a drug cartel. They're just trying to make some point with Agent Archer and probably saw him with Ms. Hart. I don't think you have anything to worry about."

Clay gave Espinoza a sharp glance. He wouldn't go that far. "Look, Meg. I'm going to get a security system installed at my house with cameras. I'll do the same for this house."

Her eyes bugged out. "Because you think this will happen again?"

"No, no, but it's not a bad idea, is it?" Clay turned to April and rolled his eyes.

Espinoza cleared his throat. "Ma'am, since you live here, can I ask you a few questions about any unusual activity you may have seen in the neighborhood starting yesterday?"

"Of course." Meg pointed a trembling finger at the box on her porch, roped off with yellow tape. "Is that it?"

"It is. We'll have it out of here shortly." Espinoza touched Meg's upper arm. "Can we talk over here?"

Meg followed Espinoza to his car.

"Well, that wasn't too bad." April scratched Denali behind one ear. "Were you ready to take her on, Denny?"

Denali's tongue lolled out of his mouth as his big eyes, one blue, one brown, looked adoringly at April. He clearly remembered her nickname for him, which Clay hadn't used since she left.

Clay coughed. "When everyone's out of here, I'm not comfortable leaving you and Meg on your own."

Hitching a thumb in the front pocket of her jeans, April said, "Does that mean you're going to assign Denali to guard duty?"

"That means I'm going to hang around for a while, if that's okay. I don't think you'll see any more trouble. I didn't, but a member of a drug cartel knows where you live and decided to put a severed head on your porch."

"I do still have my gun at the house." She tilted her head at him. "And I know how to use it because a hotshot Border Patrol agent taught me."

"It probably needs to be cleaned. Do you even have bullets for it?"

"He taught me how to do that, too, and I'll look for the bullets or buy them." She fondled Denali's ear. "But I wouldn't mind the watchdog."

Clay leveled a finger at her. "You're going to take the bodyguard along with the watchdog."

"Before, you asked me if it was okay if you stayed—now you're telling me?"

"I didn't think you'd reject my offer. I'll even pick up dinner for you two."

"You're going to make Meg very, very nervous."

April gazed past his shoulder, and he cranked his head around to watch Meg, body stiff, arms waving around as if casting a spell. She probably would cast a spell on April if she could.

"Let me handle Meg."

"Better you than me."

An hour later, the last official vehicle pulled away from the house, leaving behind the yellow police tape and some fingerprint powder on the gate and the porch.

Meg strolled down the two steps, making a wide berth around the spot where April had found the box. "When are you getting those security systems, Clay?"

"Tomorrow. I'll install yours first and then mine.

I'll get some advice, but I'm thinking cameras, motion-sensor lights, the works."

"Can you get one of those setups where I can tune in on my phone and watch what's going on?" Meg glanced at April.

"Don't look at me. I'm not going to be hanging around Paradiso much longer."

Her words pricked his heart.

"April's going to go back to Albuquerque to get the rest of her stuff, and I'm going with her."

Meg's eyes narrowed. "I thought you hightailed it out of there to help a friend in trouble. You're actually moving from Albuquerque?"

"Yes." April grabbed Clay's arm. "Clay has offered to buy us dinner tonight, Meg. I accepted on your behalf."

"I'm not going out. I'm exhausted." She jingled her keys. "I am going to move my car into the driveway, though."

"We're not going out, either. I'm getting takeout. Any preferences?"

Meg's gaze shifted from his face to April's, a crease forming between her eyes. "Because you're worried?"

"Let's just call it cautious." He held out his hand. "I'll move your car around, and then I'll get some Chinese."

"Chinese is fine. I'll eat anything, but I'm not liking this. I'll feel better when we get the cameras up and running." Meg poked April's arm. "Are you going with him, or are you going to stay here?"

"I'll stay here—me and Denali." April hunched forward and patted her thigh. "C'mon, boy. Let's go inside."

As Clay swung through the front gate, he made a half turn. "Kung pao chicken and orange peel beef for you?"

"Absolutely. You remembered."

The two women disappeared inside the house with Denali at their heels.

Clay let the gate slam behind him and murmured, "I remember everything."

Chapter Eight

Once inside the house, April rummaged through the bags she'd brought in earlier. "I did some shopping in Tucson and bought a few things."

"Seeing that head on the porch must've been horrible for you." Meg leaned her hip against the arm of the couch. "I'm sorry you found it."

April ducked her head inside one of her bags. "Would've been worse if you'd found it."

"Because I didn't see my mother murdered?" Meg clicked her tongue. "That doesn't make you immune to atrocities, April. I would think it would bring back memories and stress you out."

"Better to have all that stress going to one person instead of spreading it around." April popped up and shook out a blouse. "Pretty, isn't it?"

"Yeah, pretty." Meg shook her head. "How did the reunion with Clay go?"

April sat back on her heels, her lips twisting into a smile. "Not as well as the reunion with Denali."

The dog, hearing his name, thumped his tail but

didn't move from his spot in front of the empty fireplace.

"Can you blame him?" Meg kicked off her shoes and padded into the kitchen on bare feet. "I need a glass of wine after that horror show. You?"

"What goes with Chinese food?"

"All I drink is white, so I guess white." Meg pulled open the fridge and emerged with an open, corked bottle of wine. "Did you ever give the poor guy a reason why you ran out on the wedding? Did you *have* a reason?"

Nobody but Adam knew the real reason, and April didn't plan on revealing anything now—especially with these heads and bodies showing up.

April's hands convulsively clutched at the material of the blouse in her hands. This wave of violence couldn't have anything to do with that prior threat, could it? No, Clay had found that body by the border before she even arrived in Paradiso. Nobody had known she was going to show up here—except Adam. He'd figured it out.

"I had my reasons, Meg, and I don't want to talk about them." She plunged her hand into another bag and dangled a pair of stone-colored capris from her fingers. "Cute?"

"I'm sure they look cute on you." Meg took a swig of wine from her glass and set another on the end table for April. "Everything does."

"Aw, thanks, cuz." April gathered the bags and pushed to her feet. "I'm going to put these away, and then I'll join you for that wine."

She walked to her bedroom on knees that still trembled. As if sensing her shakiness, Denali popped up and trotted after her.

April put away the new clothes and washed her face and hands before joining Meg. Denali stayed by her side, determined to keep her in his sight. She'd missed the silly pooch almost as much as she'd missed Clay.

"Here you go." Meg thrust a glass at her as she returned to the living room.

April sat on one side of the couch, curling a leg beneath her, and cupped the wineglass with both hands.

"First, a toast." Meg raised her glass. "To no more drama."

April clinked her glass with her cousin's. "I'll drink to that."

"There's never a dull moment living down here, is there?"

"Or maybe it's just our family." April took a sip of the wine, lolling the citrusy flavor on her tongue before swallowing.

"Where are you headed once you collect your stuff from Albuquerque?"

"I'm not sure yet, maybe back to LA."

"You're not going to stick around and give Clay another chance?"

April snorted. "I'm sure Clay's finished with me."

Meg threw her head back and laughed at the ceiling. "Right. Not even Denali believes that."

The knock on the door made them both jump, and Denali scrambled to his feet.

"Must be Clay." April pointed at Denali's wagging tail. She nudged Denali aside and peered through the peephole. Swinging open the door, she said, "The man and the kung pao."

"That's me." Clay held up the bags and shuffled across the threshold, scooting Denali out of the way.

Meg turned off the TV and strolled into the kitchen. "Glass of wine?"

"Sure. I gotta tell you, word travels fast in this town."

"News of the second head out already?" April took the bags from Clay and followed Meg. Was it too soon to ask for a second glass of wine?

"Yeah, there's some grim competition going on to find the other body."

"Ugh." April swung the bags onto the counter, once again feeling her appetite recede.

"Let's talk about something else." Meg thrust a wineglass at Clay, and the golden liquid sloshed over the rim.

Clay tipped his head. "Got it."

Sitting on the floor, gathered around Meg's coffee table, the three of them managed to avoid the subject of heads, headless bodies, drugs and the border for the entirety of their meal, finishing the last of it by cracking open fortune cookies and assigning absurd meanings to the fortunes within.

Meg wiped a tear from her eye and drained her third glass of wine. "Oh, wow, I needed that."

"The wine or the laughter?" Clay tapped her glass with his chopstick.

"Both." Meg yawned. "I'm going to fall into a deep sleep tonight."

"Otherwise known as passing out." April crawled on the floor toward Meg and took her arm, pulling her up. "You go to bed. Clay and I will clean up."

"You're welcome to stay the night, Clay. Both of the extra beds are made up, or you can stay in someone else's bed." Meg gave an exaggerated wink, distorting her mouth in the process.

April's cheeks warmed, and she tugged harder at Meg's arm. "You're tipsy, cuz. Off to bed with you."

Meg giggled as she staggered to her feet and weaved down the hallway.

"Lightweight." Clay held up Meg's empty glass to the light.

"She did drink more than both of us put together." April collected the rest of the glasses and dishes. "She needed it. She comes across as feisty but the head really spooked her."

"And you?"

Clay touched her arm, the pressure of his fingertips making her weak in the knees all over again—but in a good way.

"I'm okay. I didn't see anything this time except a little blood. No more images to add to my nightmares."

"Do you still have nightmares?" The touch on her arm turned to a featherlight brush.

"Not often."

"Do you want me to stay? In another room, of course."

"I think Meg would like that. If she mentioned it, she meant it." She stepped away from the warmth that emanated from his body and carried the dishes into the kitchen.

He followed her like she knew he would and leaned against the counter. "And you?"

"I think both Meg and I would feel safer with you and Denali here tonight." She dumped the dishes in the sink. "Do you want to help me with these?"

"You rinse, and I'll put them in the dishwasher."

They worked well together, just as they always had in the past, and it all felt so natural. She wanted this again. She wanted Clay. She'd been a fool to believe Jimmy could ever replace him.

She held out the last plate. "That's it. Do you want me to search through Meg's cupboards for a toothbrush?"

As he took the plate, he curled his fingers around hers. "I missed you."

Tears pricked the backs of her eyes and she blinked. She couldn't do this with him.

She slid her hands from the plate, grabbed a dish towel and flicked it at Denali's head. "I think he did, too."

Clay's jaw tightened as he hunched over the dishwasher to put away the plate. "Don't blame me if he jumps on your bed to sleep with you tonight."

"I'd like that." April spun away from Clay. "I'd like that a lot."

Too bad he meant the dog and not him.

THE FOLLOWING MORNING, April got up when she heard Meg banging around in the kitchen. She'd barely gotten any sleep the night before, anyway—between visions of headless bodies and the thought of Clay's very real body in the next room, she couldn't turn off her mind.

She crept up behind her cousin. "How are you feeling?"

Meg yelped and dropped a coffee cup, which hit the tile floor and cracked. "Oh my God. Why are you sneaking up on me?"

"I'm sorry." April crouched down and retrieved the broken pieces of the cup. "I figured you'd have a hangover. I was trying to be quiet."

"I do have a hangover, and I still have to go to work."

April patted Meg's back. "Sit down. I'll get your coffee."

"Did you and Clay kiss and make up last night?"

"Of course not." April threw a little pink packet of sweetener at Meg. "He was here to protect us."

"Yeah, okay." Meg's eyes widened. "Good morning, Clay. Did we wake you?"

"Sounded like you two were throwing glasses around in here." He curled one arm behind his head and patted his flat belly as he yawned.

"Just an accident." April pointed to the pieces of glass on the counter. "How'd you sleep?"

"Great, without Denali crowding me. You?"

"Fine—with Denali crowding me."

Meg heaved a sigh. "Can you please pour that coffee into my commuter mug? I have to get out of here. When are you two going to Albuquerque?"

Clay answered, "Tomorrow morning. I have a few days off, but don't worry. I'll get your security system installed first."

"That would be great."

"Do you want me to leave Denali behind with you when we go to Albuquerque? He can serve as another layer of protection, and it would be easier for me and April to drive without him."

"About that." April set Meg's mug in front of her. "We'll have to take separate cars. I need to get that car back to its rightful owner."

Meg's hand jerked as she stirred the sweetener in her coffee. "Wait, you stole that car?"

"Not exactly."

Meg raised her hand. "That's enough. I'm off to work…and I'd be happy to take care of your dog."

When the front door slammed behind her, a heavy silence hung over the room.

April cleared her throat. "Do you want me to watch Denali while you're at work? We have some catching up to do."

"Are you going to stick around here all day, or do you want to stay at my place? Denali needs to eat."

"We can stay at your place, and I'll feed him." She held up her coffee mug. "Do you want some coffee?"

"No, thanks. I'll wait for you to get ready, and you can follow me over to my place. I'll shower and change there, and then leave you and Denali to your own devices."

She flicked her fingers. "You two can get a head start. I'll come over when I'm ready."

"Are you sure you're okay to stay here alone?" Clay spread his hands. "I didn't want to leave you alone."

"I won't be alone." She put her cup in the sink. "Leave Denali with me. I'm going to get my gun out, too. You can help me clean it and load it sometime today."

Someone knocked on the door and Denali growled.

"See how good he is?" April patted Denali's head on the way to answer the door, but Clay grabbed her arm. "Let me."

He leaned into the peephole and nodded. "Perfect timing. It's Charlie Santiago from Paradiso PD."

Clay opened the door. "Hey, Charlie."

"You here already, Clay? Doing some investigating?"

"No, I'm going back out to the site where we found the first body. You here to do some more canvassing?" Clay widened the door to include April in the conversation.

"Hello, Ms. Hart. I hope you and your cousin had an uneventful evening."

"It was. Clay's leaving and is nervous about my being here by myself. Can you let him know you can keep an eye on the house for the next thirty minutes or so?"

"No problem. I'll be in the neighborhood for about an hour." He adjusted his equipment belt, the leather creaking and handcuffs jingling. "I'll keep a lookout for anything suspicious."

"Problem solved." Clay winked at her. "Don't take too long."

With Clay gone, Charlie the cop patrolling the neighborhood and Denali parked outside the bathroom door, April showered, allowing the knot in her belly to loosen.

She grabbed her new purse and exited the house. She waved at Charlie in his patrol car as she patted the passenger seat of her ill-gotten vehicle and Denali jumped inside.

Before she started the engine, she tried calling Adam. Again, his phone rang without rolling over to voice mail. She tried a text and watched the display for the notification that it had been delivered. That notification never came through.

Why was he offline? Had Jimmy threatened him? Did Adam know who took Jimmy's flash drive?

Denali whined beside her and she touched his nose and said, "My brother's a mystery, Denali."

By the time she got to Clay's place, he'd already showered and changed into a fresh uniform. He'd always looked good in the Border Patrol greens that matched his hazel eyes. Hell, Clay Archer would look hot in a clown suit.

He shook a dog dish full of dry food. "I already got Denali's breakfast ready and changed his water outside. Just add a little warm water to his kibble when he's ready to eat."

"You're going to work and then to the hardware store to get the security systems?"

"Work, back here for lunch to check on you two and then to my friend's place. He installs the systems and I can get a couple from him. Will you be back here at noon?"

"I'll make sure of it. I'll even make us some lunch."

"What do you plan to do this morning?"

"I meant what I said. I'm going to get reacquainted with Denali—and try to reach my brother."

Clay raised his eyebrows. "No word from Adam?"

"Nope." She pushed her hair from her face. "Maybe he doesn't realize I called Jimmy and doesn't want to have any contact with me in case Jimmy finds out."

"You called Adam from your new phone, didn't you?"

"Yeah."

"Adam doesn't know that number. He wouldn't know to avoid it."

"I also texted him, letting him know it's me."

"Keep at it. I'm curious to find out what he knows about that flash drive."

"You'd better get going. Denali and I have things to do."

"Don't make him adore you more than he already does. You're gonna break his doggy heart when you leave again."

April swallowed hard. "Denali and I have an understanding."

"If you say so." Clay jerked his thumb over his shoulder. "I took out the supplies to clean your gun and left them on a workbench in the garage, if you're serious."

She patted the small backpack she borrowed from Meg. "Oh, I'm serious. I have my piece with me."

One corner of Clay's mouth turned up. "Okay, then you should probably clean your...piece."

"Go ahead and laugh. You know I'm a good shot."

"I know you are. Just be careful."

"With the gun...or everything else?"

"In general."

"I think the heads are just some kind of message to you. I don't think Meg and I have to worry."

"Probably not." He hitched his bag over his shoulder. "I don't like the idea that these people know you're connected to me somehow and followed you home. It means they're still here—watching."

She tightened her grip on the strap of the backpack. "I don't like it, either, but I'll be safe with Denali and my gun, once I get it ready."

"Then I'll see you at lunch." He waved on his way out the door.

April fed Denali, cleaned and loaded her gun, and then slipped into Clay's office where he had a tablet charging on his desk.

He didn't have a password on the computer, so she launched a browser and started a search for El Gringo Viejo. After scanning past a few results for Mexican restaurants, she zeroed in on a couple articles about the mysterious drug supplier in Mexico.

This guy didn't have the fame or notoriety of

some of the other big-time drug lords—no fancy villas, no fancy girlfriends. In fact, nobody knew where he lived. Nobody knew what he looked like. Nobody knew much about how he operated.

Where would Adam get the idea that El Gringo Viejo was their father? Why would he tell Jimmy? None of it made any sense.

The articles didn't provide much information, certainly not enough to head down to Mexico on a fact-finding mission. Of course, if she went down there and let the word drop in a few circles that the daughter of El Gringo Viejo was searching for him, she might just get a hit. Or take a hit.

What did she hope to accomplish by finding her father? If he really were El Gringo Viejo, wouldn't that shoot her theory all to hell that he never murdered Mom? It would, in fact, confirm his guilt.

Sighing, she slumped in the chair. She'd just gotten out of a sticky situation with Jimmy. Clay was right. She should put this all behind her and move on—put Clay behind her, too. What was the shelf life for threats? She didn't want to find out.

Denali whined at her feet, and she kicked off a sandal and ran the bottom of her foot across the soft fur on his back. "Are you ready to go for a walk, boy?"

His ears cocked forward and his tail wagged in response.

She'd missed having a dog. Jimmy had claimed he was allergic. That should've been a sign right there.

She collected Denali's leash and stuffed a plastic

bag in the pocket of her capris. She hooked him up and set out for the pecan groves about a half mile from Clay's house.

Nash Dillon's family owned this particular grove in addition to the one surrounding his house, had owned this land for years. Her sandals scuffed against the dirt, and she unclipped Denali's leash from his collar so he could roam a little bit.

April inhaled the slightly sour scent of the trees and soaked in the dry heat that seemed to permeate her skin and warm her bones. She could've been happy in Paradiso with Clay if her life hadn't taken a hard left turn her senior year of college.

If her father hadn't stabbed her mother to death in their kitchen. If her fragile little brother hadn't found the body. If she hadn't had to clean up everyone else's messes.

Denali's sharp bark pierced the air as he appeared through the trees as if chasing a rabbit—or running from something.

He skidded to a stop in front of her, the fur on his back standing on end. He twirled around to face the grove that had just spit him out. His lip curled, one tooth hooked over his lip, but he remained silent, his entire body quivering.

His fear reached out to her, causing a chill to sweep across her flesh. "What is it, boy? Something coming after you?"

She tipped her sunglasses to the edge of her nose and peered through the trees. Maybe nothing was chasing him. Maybe he'd found something.

"Did you see something? Dig something up?" She shivered despite the heat beating on her shoulders.

Could there be another head? They seemed to be following her around in this town since she arrived. Maybe not another head, but there was definitely another body out there.

Crouching down, she attached Denali's leash to his collar and gave him a little yank. She had no intention of finding a woman's headless body out here on her own.

"C'mon, Denali."

He offered no resistance, scampering ahead of her, leading her from the grove.

She glanced over her shoulder once. "You and me both, Denali. Let's see what your dad has for lunch."

By the time she reached Clay's house, her heart rate had returned to normal. All kinds of things spooked dogs. It didn't have to be a dead body.

She filled Denali's water dish and gave him a quick brush before washing her hands and inspecting Clay's kitchen. For a bachelor, he had a halfway decent supply of regular food. Yeah, he had plenty of beer and a fair number of take-out containers with questionable contents, but he did have fresh vegetables and some eggs still within their date of expiration.

She whipped up a couple of omelets and mixed a salad of tomatoes, cucumbers and avocados. By the time Clay came through the door, she'd added a vase of flowers to the kitchen table and poured two glasses of iced tea.

He swept off his hat, his gaze bouncing from the table to her face. "You didn't have to go through all this trouble."

"No trouble. I can't believe how nicely those flowers are growing out back in this weather."

"You planted them." He swung his bag onto the kitchen table and the flowers wobbled on their stems. "I just keep watering them like you told me to."

"You do have a green thumb, Clay Archer."

Holding up his thumb, he inspected it. "I'm just good at following orders."

"Well, so am I." She ignored his eye roll. "I cleaned my gun with the stuff you left in the garage, took Denali out for a walk and managed to scrape some food together for lunch."

"Looks good." He unbuckled his equipment belt, which sagged on his hips. "I'm gonna wash my hands and dig in. Called my friend with the security business. He's going to help me outfit both houses."

"I'll pay for his services at my house."

He cranked his head over his shoulder as he scrubbed his hands beneath the kitchen faucet. "We'll take care of it. I feel like I owe Meg something for bringing that to her home...your home. What is that arrangement, anyway?"

"She'll stay there until I decide if I want to sell the house or not." April pulled out a chair at the table, tucking the strap of Clay's bag beneath the satchel.

"You don't have to check with Adam?"

"Adam doesn't own the house. I do." She picked up a fork. "I—I mean I'll share the money with him if I sell it."

"Why should you?" Clay took a seat at the table and flicked the cloth napkin into his lap. "That's not what your mother intended, is it? That's why you got all her life insurance money, too. She didn't trust Adam with the money."

April nibbled on her bottom lip. "I was never able to reach him today. I want to check on him tomorrow when we go to Albuquerque."

"I sure hope Verdugo didn't find out that Adam took that flash drive."

"I don't think Adam would be that stupid to nab Jimmy's property—whatever it contains."

Clay snorted but refrained from commenting as he dug into his omelet. "Tell me about Denali's walk. Did you take him to the pecan grove?"

"Yes, but he saw something that spooked him. Ran back to me all in a tizzy, fur sticking up."

"Always happens." Clay plucked a glob of melted cheese from his plate and held it under the table for Denali.

"You spoil him."

"You should talk." Clay waved his fork over the table. "This is great, thanks."

"The least I could do." *Considering I ran out on our wedding.*

When Clay ignored Denali's demands for more table scraps, the dog scampered around the table in a big circle, sniffing the floor. On his second rotation, he crashed into the leg of the table and Clay's bag began to slip from the table.

April grabbed the strap, but Clay's heavy bag fell to the floor with a clump, anyway, a sheaf of papers sliding from the top.

"Hope he didn't break my laptop."

"It should be fine." She crouched on the floor as Clay scraped back his chair.

"I'll get that."

The papers fanned out in front of her on the floor, and she swept them into a pile and tapped them on the tile.

"I'll take those."

She glanced up at Clay's face, a little white around his pursed lips, and then shifted her gaze to the papers in her hand. She flipped the stack over, and a lump formed in her throat.

"Pictures of the head from yesterday."

"I'm sorry, yeah." Clay held out his hand. He repeated, "I'll take those."

She brought the printout of the photo close to her face and studied the gory details. Then she dropped the sheaf of papers and fell back onto the floor with a strangled cry.

"I know. I'm sorry, April. You shouldn't have looked. I told you not to look."

She brought a hand to her tight throat and her eyes met Clay's as she choked out, "I know her."

Chapter Nine

Clay snatched the printouts and crushed them to his chest where his heart thundered. "No, you just think you do. People in death don't look the same as they did in life—especially if they've been beheaded. She could be anyone."

April cranked her head back and forth, a blank stare in her blue eyes. "I know that woman. Her name is Elena."

Clay stuffed the sheaf of papers, now crinkled and creased, into his bag and took April by the hand to help her to her feet.

She rose and then immediately plopped down in her chair. If the chair hadn't been there, she would've wound up on the floor again.

She smoothed her palms over her thighs, over and over, ironing the wrinkles in her pants. "It's her. I know it's Elena."

"Here." Clay shoved the sweating iced tea glass under her nose. "Drink something."

"What does it mean? Why is she here?" April

stopped the repetitive movement and grabbed his hand, her nails clawing at his flesh.

He curled his fingers around her wrist and squeezed. "Why do you think it's this woman Elena? The features are distorted, her skin discolored. Detective Espinoza was wondering at the office how we were going to put a sketch out. That's why the sheriff's department didn't realize right away that the woman's head from the day before yesterday didn't belong to the body we found at the border. Skin color, features, sagging, wrinkling... all change under those dire conditions."

"Look again." She poked at his bag with a trembling finger. "That woman has a nose piercing."

His pulse ratcheted up another few notches. "Lots of women have nose piercings."

"Look again, Clay." She folded her hands in her lap, twisting her fingers. "The piercing is a star, a small, gold star."

Clay's tongue stuck to the roof of his dry mouth. He didn't have to look. They'd already noted the star piercing on the woman's nose.

Lifting her chin, April placed a hand over her heart. "It's true, isn't it? You've seen the piercing."

"If you do know who this is—and I'm not conceding that you do—how do you know her? Who is Elena?"

Her fingers curled against the skin of her chest. "I met her at Jimmy's."

Clay closed his eyes as a stifling dread thrummed through his veins. When he'd believed that the cartel had left the head on April's porch because of him, it had angered him. If they'd left it there so Jimmy could send some kind of message to April, that scared the hell out of him.

His lids flew open. He couldn't let April know how much her words had struck terror into his heart.

He smoothed his palms over her arms, pulling her hands away from her throat where she'd scored it with red marks from her nails. He laced his fingers with hers.

"In what capacity? What was she doing at Jimmy's?"

"Sh-she is, was, Gilbert's girlfriend."

"Gilbert is the man you overheard talking with Jimmy in his office when you were out on the balcony?"

She nodded once, dropping her chin to her chest. "What does it mean? Did Jimmy kill her or have her killed?"

She jumped up from her chair so fast and with so much force she knocked him over and he braced a hand against the floor.

She buried her hands in her hair and screamed, the sound launching Denali to his feet. "I can't believe I was with that man. I can't believe Adam would set me up like that."

Clay grabbed the edge of the table and hoisted himself up. "I'm not defending Jimmy here or trying to tell you he's a great guy, but I don't believe he had Elena murdered."

"You think it's some great, cosmic joke that I met a woman at Jimmy's who winds up murdered and beheaded at the border and her head makes it to my front porch?" She stooped down automatically and patted Denali, frantically circling her.

"Can you sit down a minute? You're making Denali and me nervous." He grabbed the back of the kitchen chair. "Sit and drink some tea. I can get you something stronger if you want."

She wedged a hand against the nearest wall and her whole frame shuddered. "The tea will do."

She crossed the room and took a seat.

He pulled the other chair around to face hers and straddled it. "Let's slow down and think a minute. Jimmy belongs to Las Moscas, right? You saw the wooden tokens in his desk drawer. He wouldn't have those for any other reason than that he belongs to that cartel."

"That's right, and you told me Elena had one of those clutched in her cold, lifeless hand."

Clay huffed out a breath. April was going to get herself wound up again. "She did, but the other agents and I never believed that she was one of Las Moscas' mules. They killed her and left that token in her hand as a warning to others not to mess with Las Moscas."

"Mess with them? As in work against them?" She tucked the shimmering strands of her hair behind one ear as her eyes began to lose their glassiness.

"We interpreted the whole ugly scene as another gang moving into Las Moscas territory and Las Moscas reclaiming that territory in the most brutal way possible."

"You think Elena was working for a rival to Las

Moscas and that Jimmy and Gilbert are those rivals?"

"I have a strong suspicion that's what happened."

"And why me?" She finally made a grab for the iced tea glass, almost knocking it over. She saved it and took a long gulp. "Why leave her head on my porch? I didn't even realize Jimmy knew about that house."

"You can be sure Adam told him all about you. Perhaps he even told him about me."

"That's bad, Clay. That's really bad news." She grabbed the back of his chair. "What if he thinks I'm over here giving you all kinds of information about him and his operation?"

That's exactly what he feared.

Shaking her head back and forth, her brow creasing, she said, "He was stupid to leave Elena's head on my porch, knowing I could identify her."

"That's just it. Jimmy wouldn't kill his own mules. He didn't leave the head on your porch— Las Moscas did."

April blinked her wide eyes. "That's so much worse. It's terrifying enough to deal with an evil that you know, but Las Moscas? Do you think they tracked me down through Jimmy?"

"If Jimmy was part of the cartel, I'm guessing somebody in Las Moscas knows all about his relationships."

She clasped her hands, which had finally stopped trembling, between her knees. "What now?"

"Do you know Elena's last name?"

"I don't. Never heard it. I know Gilbert's, though. His is Stanley. Gilbert Stanley."

"He's not Latino?"

"He is." She jabbed a finger at his chest. "Half, like you."

"When you met Elena, was she in the company of an older, white woman?"

"She was not."

"Do you think the girlfriend story could've been a cover, or do you really believe she and Gilbert were a couple?"

"I don't have any idea. I didn't spend much time with them. She did go into Jimmy's office one time and I did wonder why she was in there when I had never been. They must've been giving her instructions then." She tapped her fingernails on the glass, rocking the slivers of ice left in the tea. "You're going to have to turn all this info over to Detective Espinoza, aren't you?"

"Of course. He needs to ID those heads."

"That means you're going to have to tell him how you know the name of the woman with the pierced nose. You're going to have to tell him that I know Jimmy Verdugo and was present in his house when he was plotting some kind of hijacking of Las Moscas."

He balanced his chin on the back of the chair. None of this would look good for April. "Maybe we can come up with a different story—just a different reason for your presence in that house."

"We can't do that, Clay. Once Espinoza talks to Gilbert…and Jimmy, they're going to tell him about me. And once he talks to them, Jimmy's going to know that I know about his business. It'll probably convince him that I stole that flash drive, too."

Massaging his throbbing temple, Clay said, "Then we don't tell Espinoza about your involvement at all."

"How are you going to explain that you happen to know the first name of a woman who wound up dead at the border?"

He shrugged, feigning a nonchalance he didn't feel. "I come in contact with a lot of mules, drug dealers, users, you name it. I'll say I came in contact with her before—remembered the nose piercing, remembered her name but nothing else."

"How is Espinoza going to tie Elena to Gilbert Stanley? He needs that connection to do a full investigation."

"I'll think of something. I don't want you involved any more than you are."

"Which is a lot, isn't it?" She stacked the plates on the table. "You need to get going on those security systems. Meg won't be happy if hers isn't in place before we leave for New Mexico."

"I'm going to tell Espinoza Elena's name first. The sooner he knows, the better. I'll do it on my way to Kyle's, my friend in security." He cocked his head. "Do you want to come with me? You'll have to keep quiet about Elena, though. Can you do that?"

As the words left his lips, he acknowledged their obviousness. April kept secrets better than anyone he knew.

Her eyebrows formed a V over her nose. "I don't want you to get into trouble covering for me."

"It's not like Espinoza isn't going to get the information we know. He is. The kind of trouble I'd be facing is nothing compared to the kind of trouble you'd be facing from Jimmy if he catches on that you know more than you're claiming to know. You're not out of the woods with that guy yet. This would put you firmly back in those woods—up a tree."

"Two years ago, you would've been happy to see me twist in the wind." Her bottom lip trembled, and he placed the pad of his thumb against the plump middle.

"Never. I never wanted anything but the best for you, April."

"Same. It's just that I knew the best for you wasn't me."

A spark ignited in his heart. Was that why she'd left him? Some stupid notion that because her father had been suspected of murdering her mother and her brother had gone off the rails after finding her body that she wasn't good enough for him?

"Did you…?"

She put up one hand. "Let's leave it. I'll clean up while you change into civilian clothes, and we'll break the news to Detective Espinoza together."

The spark he'd felt earlier died out, but he stoked it with hope that they could return to this conversation.

"Okay, just put the dishes in the dishwasher and leave the pan in the sink. I'll take care of it later."

He pushed to his feet and strode to his bedroom to change out of his uniform.

An hour later, they pulled into the parking lot of the Paradiso PD and asked for Detective Espinoza inside.

Espinoza came bustling out of a back office, his cowboy boots clomping on the tile floor. "We ID'd the young Latina."

April grabbed on to Clay's belt loops in the back and tugged

"That was fast. Who is she, and what's her story?" Clay crossed his arms over the folder with Elena's picture.

"Her name is Elena Delgado. We got a hit on her fingerprints for a couple of car thefts."

April's hold loosened. "So, she had a record?"

"Enough of one to have her prints on file, and those cases gave us an accomplice, too." Espinoza rubbed his hands together. "I'm guessing he's involved in this latest scheme that got his girlfriend killed."

"Elena has a boyfriend somewhere?" Clay shifted from one foot to the other.

"Jesus Camarena." Espinoza flicked open another file folder and jabbed his finger at the picture of a young Latino with a mustache. "Every crime that girl committed was in the presence of Camarena."

April seemed to freeze behind him. Even her breathing stopped.

Clay asked, "Where's Camarena now?"

"That's the big mystery. His name hasn't popped

up in a while." Espinoza scratched his chin. "Last known address we have for him is in Phoenix."

April sighed, the air warm against the back of Clay's neck. "Maybe he got a new identity. Changed his name to start out with a clear record."

Clay jerked, and he reached back to tap April's leg. They'd just been handed a present and she wanted to throw it back in Espinoza's face.

The detective hunched his shoulders. "Maybe, but we're gonna track him down one way or the other to find out his role in this mess. We have another person to ID."

"You're going to have to find the body to get her prints or wait for the DNA test results, but if she hasn't been arrested for a felony, her DNA isn't going to tell you much." Clay brushed the back of his hand across his forehead.

"The name Elena Delgado mean anything to you, Archer?" Espinoza narrowed his eyes, his gaze dropping to the folder in Clay's hand.

"Nope." Clay cranked his head back and forth. He held up the folder. "I was going to tell you she looked familiar to me from the photos of the head, but features in that condition are hard to distinguish."

"Just wondering why Las Moscas went to the trouble to leave one head on your porch and the other on your... Ms. Hart's."

"They want Border Patrol to back off." Clay smacked the folder against his hand. "They've sent us messages before—just not this extreme."

"Extreme times call for extreme measures." Espinoza wagged his finger between him and Clay. "I've been up front with you. You can be up front with me. Quid pro quo and all that. I've heard Las Moscas is stepping up its shipments across the border, financed more tunnels. They've monopolized some provider in Mexico."

"El Gringo Viejo." Clay's eye twitched.

"The old gringo—yeah, that's the name I heard. Any idea who that is?"

April sucked in a soft breath beside him, and he shrugged. "We don't know. Probably some old, white guy."

"Brilliant deduction, Archer." Espinoza clapped Clay on the back with a chuckle. "Why did you come in to see me?"

Clay waved the folder in front of him. "Just to tell you the woman looked familiar, but you beat me to the punch."

"We'll keep you posted on the drug angle if we get anything from this Camarena. That poor little lady didn't have a chance once she joined forces with that guy."

"And we'll keep you up to date on any activities at the border that might relate to this case." Clay made a half turn, putting his hand on the small of April's back. "I'll be out of town for the next few days. You have my contact info if something comes up."

"Agent Dillon's out of pocket, too. You're leaving me with that green kid, Valdez?"

"Put him through some paces. He'll be fine."

Once outside, April heaved a huge sigh, her shoulders slumping. "That was a piece of luck. We just had to lie by omission. We didn't have to flat out lie."

"There's a difference?" He raised one eyebrow. "Is this the world according to April?"

A pink blush rushed into her cheeks, and she turned away. "I'm glad they ID'd Elena Delgado. Do you think they'll track down Jesus, aka Gilbert?"

"So, that was him in the booking photo of Camarena that Espinoza showed us?"

"You couldn't tell by my reaction? I almost passed out."

"Yeah, I noticed." Clay grabbed the handle of the passenger door and paused. "Detective Espinoza could get an anonymous tip about a certain house in Albuquerque."

"It's totally possible that the cops would track down Gilbert after identifying Elena, right? Jimmy wouldn't necessarily suspect me of dropping a dime on them. Besides, Jimmy has no idea that Elena's head was left on my porch. Las Moscas isn't going to tell him anything."

"Jimmy has bigger problems than a runaway bride right now. He's probably sweating bullets wondering if his bosses in the cartel are going to tie him and Gilbert to the two mules trying to poach Las Moscas' shipment."

April leaned her hip against the car door. "They'll kill him, won't they?"

"If what they did to those two women is any indication of the wrath of Las Moscas, I wouldn't want to be in Jimmy's shoes right now." Not that he wasn't in Jimmy's shoes just two years ago when April had run out on their wedding. He popped open the door and held it open for her.

She started to slide in and then grabbed the doorjamb. "Are you wondering why I agreed to marry Jimmy so quickly?"

Clay clenched his jaw. "I think we established you were looking for some security and Adam had coached Jimmy into being the perfect man for you."

Clay had always believed he was the perfect man for April, and he couldn't imagine anyone less like him than a drug dealer.

"At the beginning…he was just like you." She dropped onto the seat and pulled the car door closed.

LATER THAT AFTERNOON, April stood on the walkway leading to her house, squinting at Clay and Kyle Lewis on ladders adjusting the cameras.

When Clay started his descent, she lunged forward and grabbed the ladder to steady it, enjoying the view of his backside as he made his way down.

She shifted to the side, and he jumped to the ground, his tool belt clanking around his waist.

"When Meg gets home, we'll have her test it out on her phone. I don't expect any more body parts to appear at your house, but I think this will make Meg feel a little better."

"One hundred percent." She darted toward the other ladder as Kyle made his way down.

"Are you ready for that beer now?"

"Absolutely. Let me clean up the site first."

April left Clay and Kyle to fold up the ladders, collect the packaging and put away their tools as she went into the house and got two bottles of beer and a can of diet soda from the fridge.

When Meg got home from work, Kyle showed her how to call up the security cam on her cell and they spent so much time with their heads together huddled over the phone April caught Clay's eye and jerked her head to the side.

Clay stood up and stretched. "April and I are going outside to check the sensors again. Let us know if something's not working."

Kyle glanced up, a surprised look on his face as if he'd forgotten their presence. "Yeah, sure."

Clay held the door open for her and they crowded on one side of the porch, away from where she'd discovered the head. He grabbed her hand. "Let's wander among the cacti."

She left her hand in his as they meandered along the brick pathway that wended through the garden of succulents. Small fairy lights cast a twinkling glow on their way.

The tears in April's eyes blurred the lights, turning them into a shimmering river. She sniffed and Clay squeezed her fingers.

"Your mother had a lot of imagination and charm. You must miss her."

"I do." She flung her arm out to the side. "Especially when I'm in this place she loved so much." She stopped and tapped the toe of her sandal against the wooden border that separated the path from the plants. "I wish I could talk to my father about what happened and why."

Clay swung around and grabbed her shoulders. "Don't get any crazy ideas about going south to find El Gringo Viejo. He's not your father, and if he were, what could he tell you? He murdered your mother because she found out about his involvement in the drug trade?"

"Why kill her if he were going to run away, anyway? Why not just run away to Mexico and disappear, like he did?"

"Maybe it was a crime of passion. Your mother confronted him, and he killed her." Clay's fingers dug into her flesh until she rolled her shoulders, and he dropped his hands. "Sorry."

"That's what I want to know."

"I can understand why you have questions, but it's not safe to track down your father—if you could. Law enforcement hasn't been able to find him. C. J. Hart was even featured on one of those most-wanted crime shows."

"The FBI received a lot of tips from that show."

"Lots of tips that led nowhere. Do you really think you can do better?"

"I'm his daughter. He'll want me to find him."

"Will he?"

April drew a circle in the dirt with her toe. Why would her father want to see her? If he weren't guilty, he would've contacted her by now to try to explain. All these years and not one word.

She blew out a breath. "You're right."

"Do you want me to spend the night again? We can get an early start for Albuquerque." He jerked his thumb over his shoulder.

"That's okay. We have our security system now, and I'll be up early." She tugged on his sleeve. "Denali's waiting for you."

"I would've brought him back with me, along with his food and toys, for Meg."

April's phone rang, and she held up a finger to Clay. "Hold that thought. Thank God, it's Adam."

She tapped the display. "Adam, where have you been? I've been calling you."

"April?"

The breathy female voice stirred the hair on the back of April's neck. "Kenzie?"

"Yeah, it's me. You haven't heard from Adam, either?"

"What are you doing with his phone? Where is he?" April pressed the phone against her chest and said to Clay, "It's Adam's girlfriend."

Kenzie choked out a sob. "I don't know where he is, April. I haven't heard from him since the day of the wedding. I finally decided to come over to your place to look for him. I didn't find him here, but I found his phone, turned off, and...blood. April, there's so much blood."

Chapter Ten

Clay glanced at April in the passenger seat of his truck and brushed his knuckle down her arm. "We'll find him."

"Will we? Jimmy must've taken him. Adam told me Jimmy was after him. I guess he got him." She clamped a hand down on her bouncing knee.

"Maybe he thinks Adam took that flash drive." Clay reached for his cup of coffee and took a sip, although the lukewarm liquid tasted more like vinegar than coffee. "Are you sure you don't want to call the Albuquerque police?"

"We can't do that, Clay. Kenzie didn't want to touch the drugs Adam left behind at my place, and I can't blame her. Can you imagine if the police showed up at the apartment to check out the scene and found all those drugs…at *my* apartment?"

"So, we go out there and get rid of the drugs first and *then* call the police? That's not gonna look good, either."

"It won't look good if they know about the drugs." She poked his thigh. "You're Border Patrol. You have contacts in the DEA. Tell them about the drugs if you want to dispose of them legally."

"What quantity of drugs are we talking about? Did Kenzie tell you what was lying around?"

"No. She was practically hysterical by the time she got off the phone with me when she realized I haven't talked to Adam since the day of the wedding, either. I didn't get much out of her."

"How'd she get into your place?"

"It was open. The front door was unlocked."

"Great." A muscle jumped at the corner of his mouth. "Adam brought his drugs to your place, and Jimmy scooped him up there—and not without a struggle. There's a reason why Jimmy left the drugs in your apartment instead of taking them."

"And it worked. He knew I wouldn't call the police—and I'm not." April drew lines on the thighs of her pants as she raked her fingernails up and down her legs. "I hope Adam doesn't have that flash drive. Jimmy will kill him—if he hasn't already."

"Depends on what's on the flash drive. If Jimmy gets it back from Adam, he might decide to use it against him. He just lost two mules."

April crossed her hands over her chest. "You think Jimmy will use Adam to intercept drugs from Las Moscas?"

"I don't know, April. It's one possibility." His hands clenched the steering wheel. "You shouldn't be rushing back into this mess. You don't owe your brother a thing after what he did to you—after what he's done to you."

Flicking her fingers in the air, she said, "I was coming here, anyway, although I wish I could've driven that car to return it to Ryan."

"With Adam missing and drugs and blood in your apartment, we didn't have time to make a detour to a location you may or may not remember." He made a grab for the cup again and knocked it from the cup holder."

"Nothing spilled." April plucked it off the floor and squeezed his bicep. "Don't worry. I have you by my side, and I can't leave Adam hanging out to dry."

He kept his mouth shut and ground his teeth instead of talking. He'd said it all before about Adam, and April didn't want to hear it. She claimed he didn't understand because he was an only child. That could be it, but looking at her relationship with Adam made him glad he didn't have siblings.

They made a few stops on the way to Albuquerque and arrived at April's apartment by one o'clock in the afternoon. When they pulled into her empty parking space in the garage, April wedged her hands against the dashboard.

"My car's gone."

"We can add grand theft auto to the list of crimes we're gonna report." Clay withdrew his weapon as he got out of the car. "I doubt Jimmy's going to come back here if he's the one who took your brother, but the guy sounds desperate at this point. No telling what he might do."

April exited the car and stretched her arms over her head. "I'm not waiting down here. It's dark and

Jimmy knows where my parking space is, even if I no longer have a car."

"Just don't go charging into your place. Did Kenzie lock up when she left?"

"She doesn't remember, but I hope not." She slammed her door and came around to his side. "I don't have the keys to my place."

Clay followed April upstairs to her apartment, and then squeezed past her when they reached her door. "Let me."

He placed his ear against the solid wood, curling his fingers around the door handle. He twisted it and said over his shoulder, "It's still unlocked."

"At least I don't have to break into my own place."

"You don't have a manager on-site?"

"No, just a number to call for the management company." She tipped her head at the door. "Are we going in?"

"Me first." He eased open the door, his muscles tight, his finger on the trigger of his gun.

The door squeaked softly on its hinges. Clay tilted his head back and sniffed the air. Didn't smell like blood—or death.

He took a step into the living room, April clinging to the waistband of his jeans, her staccato breathing pulsing behind him. He swiveled his head back and forth, taking in the small room. "How many rooms?"

"This one, the kitchen, one bathroom and two bedrooms." She nudged his arm. "Down the hall that way."

Clay crept into the room, his gun at his side while April stayed behind. He poked his head into the kitchen and veered to the left and the short hallway. All three doors stood wide open, and he entered each room and checked the two closets.

He strode back into the living room, making a wide arc with one hand. "Where is all this blood Kenzie saw?"

"Not sure." From the living room behind the couch, April held her arms out to her sides, several plastic bags clutched in her hands. "But here are the drugs. Looks like crystal meth and weed."

Clay holstered his gun, shut and locked the front door. "You don't need anyone seeing you with that stuff."

April dropped the bags on the console table behind the couch and put her hands on her hips. "I'm a little relieved. I expected the place to be turned over with blood soaking the carpet and packets of drugs."

Clay peered over the counter that separated the kitchen from the living room. "It's in here, April, the blood."

She appeared next to him in a flash, her face white, her eyes round. "It—it looks smeared. Do you think Kenzie tried to clean it up?"

"Looks like someone did." He patted her back. "Stay here."

He circled around the counter, avoiding the blood spots on the floor. More blood spatters decorated the inside of the sink and droplets had dried on the granite countertop.

"Someone washed up in the sink. Until we question Kenzie, we don't know if she tried to clean up or if this blood belongs to the assailant. Why did she assume this was Adam's blood?"

"His phone was here, turned off, and his drugs. Who else would have access to my apartment?"

Clay cleared his throat. "Uh, your fiancé."

"He never came here." Two splotches of red splashed her cheeks. "He doesn't have a key."

"Trash?" He nudged an elongated drawer with his toe. When she nodded, he pulled it open and tossed the garbage at the top with his fingers. "I don't see any paper towels or rags in here covered with blood. Do you have a laundry room?"

"Not in here. I can't imagine Kenzie cleaning up and then taking a bunch of bloody towels to the washing machines downstairs."

"You need to get her back on the phone and find out exactly what she saw when she came in here. This scene—" he waved his arms around the kitchen "—doesn't make much sense."

April took a wide stance in the middle of the room. "After I ran out on the wedding, Adam must've gone to Jimmy's, anyway. Maybe that's when Jimmy threatened him…and me. Adam picked up my purse with my keys and let himself into my place."

"That's your purse?" Clay pointed to a large bag on the coffee table that looked more like a small suitcase.

"That's the bag I brought with me to Jimmy's to get ready for the wedding." April swooped down to grab it and dug inside, a few of the contents falling to the floor in her haste. She twirled a key chain around her finger. "Keys."

"Car keys?"

"Yeah, but Adam has his own set of keys to my car."

"What did Adam do next, detective?" Clay crossed his arms and wedged a hip against the couch.

"He dropped off my stuff…"

"And brought his drugs."

She sucked in her bottom lip. "Maybe he just scored."

"Nice of him to bring them here." He held up his hands as she opened her mouth. "I don't know how we're going to locate Adam without the help of the police."

April snapped her fingers and pointed her finger at him. "Detective Espinoza should be contacting Gilbert…or Jesus. Maybe that will make Jimmy and his gang nervous enough that they'll release Adam."

"I wouldn't count on Jimmy getting spooked at this point by a few inquiries into Elena. Do you think Jimmy would take Adam to his house?"

"Maybe. What are you thinking?" April brushed her hands together as if to erase the drugs.

"You can't go out to Jimmy's place, but I can— just for a surveillance. I can check things out, and Jimmy won't even know I'm there."

"Except—" April skirted the couch, hitching her purse over her shoulder "—Jimmy has security cameras."

"As you found out, I happen to have a good friend in security and I know how to disable any system. I'm not going in with guns blazing. I'm just gonna see what I can see."

"I'm going with you." She sliced a hand in the air through his objections. "I'll stay out of sight, but first let's finish the cleanup."

"Do you have any cotton swabs and plastic bags? I want to take a sample of this blood in the kitchen and in the sink."

"I do."

They spent the next hour collecting blood samples and cleaning up. When they finished, Clay handed April's phone to her. "Try calling Kenzie again."

As Clay took out the trash, April called Kenzie on Adam's phone. She didn't remember Kenzie's own number. The call rolled over to voice mail, but April decided not to leave a message. She didn't trust that phone and didn't much trust Kenzie, either. That girl was flakier than a Paris pastry.

Clay returned to the apartment, rubbing his hands together. "I'm just going to wash up, and I'm going to flush those drugs down the toilet while I'm at it. You finish packing your stuff and we'll get something to eat. I want the cover of darkness on my side when we go out to Jimmy's place."

April packed the stuff she wanted to take back with her to Paradiso. She'd officially give notice and move out once everything was settled with Jimmy and she'd found Adam—dead or alive.

She said, "I know a good barbecue place where we can pass the time. It's not far from Jimmy's."

"He's not going to suddenly show up there, is he?"

"Too down-home for him. He prefers upscale steak houses and cocktail lounges."

They loaded her bags and suitcases in the truck, and she directed him to Benny's Big-Time BBQ.

An hour later, seated across from each other with a pile of ribs between them, April asked, "What's your plan?"

"I'll sneak onto the grounds, disable the security system, if I have to, and surveil the scene. See who's there, including Adam."

"You're not going to know who's who without me."

"Draw me some pictures." He aimed a rib bone at her. "If I get caught, I can make up some story. If you're with me, that story's gonna be a lot different."

"You know what Gilbert looks like, right? You remember the booking photo of Jesus that Espinoza showed us. That's pretty close, except Gilbert added a goatee to that moustache." She tore open a wet wipe package and dangled the wipe from her fingers. "Do you think Espinoza has already contacted Gilbert?"

"Probably not. If he wants to do any kind of search when he finds him, he'll have to secure a warrant. It's going to take him a few days before he can formally question Gilbert and search his possessions."

"Then Jimmy and his cohorts won't know anything."

"They'll know their mules didn't make it. I'm sure

they had some sort of communication set up for when the women got across with the drugs. If he never heard from them, he'd know something went wrong."

"The heads were in the news. If he cared to check, he'd find that out." She swiped the last bit of barbecue sauce from her fingers and crumpled the wipe in her hand. "Did those news reports mention any names—like mine?"

"No, the location of the recovered heads was kept out of the news. Jimmy shouldn't know that you're involved in this at all. Even the identification of Elena can be explained by her fingerprints and her police record connecting her to Jesus." Clay dug his fork into his potato salad. "I suppose Jimmy knows you're from Paradiso if Adam already told him the story about your father."

"He knows that…but not much else—at least, not from me." She'd never told Jimmy about Clay. It had seemed almost sacrilegious to share any details of her and Clay's relationship with anyone else.

She couldn't imagine Adam would've told Jimmy that his fiancée had once been engaged to a Border Patrol agent. That wouldn't have meshed with Adam's plans of securing himself a drug-dealing brother-in-law.

Clay grabbed her hand with his sticky one. "Are you okay? Are you sure you want me to do this?"

"Yes. I'm just surprised you're willing to go to these lengths to find Adam. I know he's not your favorite person."

"He's not my favorite person because I don't like

how he twists you all up. Look, I'm sorry the kid found his mother like that, but you don't owe him a lifetime of chances because of it. He needs to get off drugs and start seeing a good therapist." Clay disentangled his fingers from hers and handed her another wet wipe. "Sorry."

"I've told Adam that a million times. He tried therapy once or twice, but it didn't work for him." She shrugged. Adam was the only immediate family she had left. She couldn't sit by and watch him self-destruct, but she'd never get pulled into one of his schemes again, and she should've recognized the setup with Jimmy as a scheme. She hadn't been thinking clearly at the time. She hadn't been thinking clearly since the day she left Clay.

"You're familiar with rock bottom, right?" Clay shoved his plate to the center of the table and planted his elbows on the linoleum.

"Yes, of course." She'd even hit it herself maybe once or twice.

"Adam hasn't hit yet because you won't allow him to. That's why he can't hear the therapist. That's why he can't get clean. You're not doing him any favors, April."

"And yet here you are ready to rush into danger to save him."

"I'm not doing this for him." Clay's eyes glowed with an intensity that made her stomach flip-flop.

She wrenched her gaze away from his and tapped the window. "Is it dark enough for you?"

"It will be once I take a bath with these wet

wipes and pay the bill." He ripped open another little packet and scrubbed his hands. "You direct me to Jimmy's and a place to park where we won't stand out. I'll go in on foot and do some reconnaissance. I'll keep my phone on vibrate, so you can serve as an early warning system in case someone comes."

"What if someone's already there? What if a lot of someones are there? What if they have Adam?"

"That's a lot of what-ifs." He raised one finger in the air at the waiter. "We'll play it by ear. I told you, I'm not going to charge in there like a super-agent. If Adam's there and it looks like he's in danger, we'll call the cops."

"All right. I'll let you call the shots, but you need to listen to me. I know these people."

"Don't remind me." He plucked the check from the waiter's hand.

"While you're paying up, I'm going to wash my hands. I feel like I have barbecue sauce under my fingernails."

Clay squinted at his nails. "You probably do."

Back in the truck, April took a deep breath. "I hope this crazy plan of yours yields some results."

"You're accusing me of crazy plans? The woman who ran out on two weddings?"

She placed a hand on her belly. "If I hadn't run out on that second one, where would I be now? Probably scrabbling through some tunnel beneath the border with Las Moscas in my future."

"Where would you have been if you hadn't run out on the first one?" Clay didn't wait for an answer to his rhetorical question, instead cranking on the engine to his truck and peeling away from the curb.

April guided him to Jimmy's compound. When he turned on the actual street of houses set back from the curb, gates and long driveways protected the residents from curious eyes and casual passersby.

With her hands stuffed beneath her thighs, she tipped her head forward. "I'm going to slump down in my seat. Drive to the end of the cul-de-sac so you can get an idea of the layout and a sense of the house and grounds."

"How long is the street from this point to the end of the cul-de-sac?"

"Less than a quarter of a mile." She loosened her seat belt and scooted down. "The houses are not cheek and jowl. There's some space between them."

"Is that how Jimmy was able to operate in relative privacy?"

"Uh-huh." The car veered to the right and her head bumped the glass. "After this bend in the road, Jimmy's place is on the left. He has a tall white gate around his property, and you can't see the house from the road."

"Got it in my sights."

"Is it all lit up?"

"Nope." Clay twisted his head to the side. "Some lights on the gate and softer lights down the driveway. Does he have sensor lights?"

"Not that I recall."

Clay swung the car around. "What's out there past the end of the cul-de-sac?"

"Nothing. Fields."

"I'll keep that in mind." He didn't slow down again on his way past the house. "Plenty of pickup trucks, so mine isn't going to stick out. Do you think it's okay to park at the top of the road? You'll have a view of who's coming in and out."

"You should be fine. Leave the keys in case I have to make a quick getaway." She pinched his thigh. "Not that I plan to leave you in the lurch or anything."

"By all means, leave me in the lurch. Like I said, I can always come up with some story." He hunched forward in his seat and pulled his wallet free from his pocket and tossed it in the console. "I'm not going to be caught with my badge and ID, either."

"But you're keeping your weapon."

"Have to. It might just get me out of trouble." He pulled into a dark space on the curb between two big, gated houses.

"Or get you into trouble."

"Don't worry, April. I know what I'm doing."

"I'm glad someone does because this is feeling more and more like a wild-goose chase."

"Have some faith in me." He threw the car into Park and left the keys swinging from the ignition. "You never did."

"Never did what?" She glanced across at him, her chin pinned to her chest.

"Had faith in me. You never had faith in me, April." He slipped from the car and pushed the door shut.

She popped up in her seat and tried to catch his

silhouette in the rearview mirror, but he'd disappeared in the night, melding with the darkness.

She waited several more minutes and exited the car on silent feet. She had no intention of letting Clay creep into the lion's den on his own. Her brother, her problem.

Hunching forward, she kept to the hedges along the dirt that functioned as a sidewalk.

When she reached Jimmy's house, she squeezed through the end of the gate and some bushes, the needling branches scratching her arms. She stumbled to a stop in the sudden darkness.

Either Clay had gotten to work already, or Jimmy had sensed company and killed the lights outside. But why would he do that? Wouldn't he turn on the floodlights to expose the intruder?

Her gaze turned to the corners of the house where she figured Jimmy's security had stationed the cameras. Had Clay disabled them?

She dropped to her hands and knees near the porch and peered into the cloak of darkness that enveloped the house. The strangeness of the scene caused pinpricks of fear to assault the back of her neck.

Even when Jimmy went out of town, he didn't leave the house in complete darkness. Clay wouldn't have been foolish enough to cut off the power to the whole house. That would alert Jimmy and his goons, and if they had Adam, they wouldn't fall for the trick and fan out to find the perpetrator. They'd be on high alert.

She rose to a crouch and circled around the

side of the house to the big windows on the great room that commanded a view of the valley. Nobody stopped her. Nothing tripped her up. She had a wide-open path.

Her heart thundered in her chest, causing a muted pounding in her ears. She dropped to the ground again when she got close to the window and a yellow glow of light from a lamp in the room.

She army-crawled on her belly across the wooden deck until her nose almost touched the cool glass of the window. Jimmy had fled. The guards, the henchmen, the security system…all demobilized.

Maybe Clay had been wrong. Perhaps Espinoza had paid a visit to Jimmy's compound looking for the man she knew as Gilbert and spooked them all into hiding. Of course, they'd fear Las Moscas finding out they were behind the double-cross more than they'd fear the law.

She hoisted herself up, curling her legs beneath her. As her eyes adjusted to the low light in the great room, she detected movement.

She held her breath, freezing in place, every muscle clenched into stillness. Then her breath hitched in her throat and her eyes widened to take in the sight of Clay bending over the dead body of Jimmy.

Chapter Eleven

April gasped, throwing out her hand to keep her balance and hitting the door, her ring scraping the glass.

Clay's head jerked up. He leveled his gun at her.

She staggered to her feet, waving her arms above her head. With her heart beating a mile a minute, she grabbed the handle of the slider.

Clay made a wide berth around Jimmy on the floor and yanked open the door. He reached through the space and dragged her inside. "What the hell are you doing here?"

"What the hell are *you* doing here? You killed Jimmy?" She shook off his hand and covered her mouth. "This is bad. This is so bad."

"Just stop." He pressed a finger against her lips. "I didn't kill Jimmy. He was dead when I got here."

Her relief caused the blood to rush to her head, and she pressed her fingertips against her temple. "Oh my God. H-how did he die?"

"Someone stabbed him to death."

She poked her head around Clay's frame and

took in the saturation of blood on the Persian carpet, giving Jimmy a halo in death that he certainly never had in life.

"Is there anyone else here? Dead or alive?" She hoped there were no live ones…dead ones, either.

"There's no one here. I could see in an instant the house was deserted, so I slipped inside. As soon as I entered this room, I could smell the blood." Clay's nostrils flared.

April sniffed the air and then wished she hadn't. Once you smelled that odor of liquid metal, you couldn't get it out of your head—or your mouth.

She ran her tongue over her teeth. "Is there any sign of a struggle throughout the house? Any sign of Adam?"

"No Adam. Struggle?" He cranked his head from side to side. "I don't see it."

"Las Moscas." She clasped her hands in front of her, twisting her fingers. "They must've found out Jimmy was the one who sent those mules and then took care of business, but where are the others? Jimmy always had an entourage."

"Maybe Las Moscas took care of them, too, and their bodies are elsewhere. Maybe some of them convinced Las Moscas they didn't know about the betrayal, and the cartel took them back into the fold."

"Where's Adam, Clay?" She rubbed the goose bumps from her arms. "Now I'm more worried than ever. At least Adam had a relationship with Jimmy. If Adam did take that flash drive and gave it back to Jimmy, Jimmy might show some mercy. But Las Moscas? They don't show mercy, do they?"

"No." He holstered the gun that had been dangling at his side all this time. "We need to talk to Kenzie to get a clearer picture of what went down at your apartment. We'll leave this mess to the police. When Espinoza comes looking for Jesus or Gilbert or whatever he's calling himself, it's going to lead him to Jimmy Verdugo and it'll be up to the Albuquerque PD to process this crime scene."

She clutched the neckline of her shirt. "We need to get rid of our fingerprints."

"I've been doing that." He pointed at the sliding glass door. "Let's take care of those—yours and mine—on the door and be careful not to touch anything else, not that your prints won't be in this house."

"They will be, along with dozens of others. Jimmy had people coming in and out of this house all the time."

"But at least your prints don't have to be anywhere near the crime scene." Clay bunched up his black T-shirt in his hand and wiped down the handle of the sliding glass door, inside and out. "Did you touch the glass?"

"No." Her gaze darted to Jimmy on the floor, his head turned to the side, his handsome face in profile. "Clay, did you see a murder weapon?"

"Nothing." He slid the door closed and flicked the lock.

"There's so much blood on the floor. How do you know he was stabbed instead of shot?"

"He was like this when I came into the room—on his back. I didn't see any wounds, so I nudged him up and saw the carnage on his back and neck, slashing wounds that ripped his clothing. Also—" he aimed a toe at Jimmy's chest "—there's no exit wound. A bullet would've exited out his front."

She swallowed. "But no knife."

"Not that I can see. Las Moscas must've sent someone Jimmy knew for him to turn his back on the guy." He ran a hand up her arm. "I'm sorry. This must bring back memories of your mother and that other crime scene. Let's get out of here."

"Not yet." She scanned the familiar room where nothing seemed out of place except the owner's body on the floor. "I want to make sure Jimmy doesn't have any pictures of me around the house. The police may make the connection between me and Jimmy soon enough, but I don't have to make it easy for them, do I?"

"In my search of the house, I found it devoid of any personal touches. Who knows if he really owns it? Who knows if his name is really Jimmy Verdugo? I'm sure you already know, a search on that name doesn't return much."

"His entire life could've been a fake." She shivered and clenched her teeth against the chill washing over her flesh. "And I could've been a part of it all. What plans do you think he had for me?"

"If Adam was spreading lies about El Gringo

Viejo being C. J. Hart, Jimmy probably wanted an introduction and a special deal for producing meth."

"For Adam to go that far, setting me up with Jimmy, he has to have some proof about our father."

Clay snorted. "Adam could've been playing Jimmy, too. Who knows? Maybe that's why Jimmy snatched him. He found out about all his lies. Do what you have to do here, and then let's bounce."

"Okay, I want to check his office. Did you go in there?"

"I did and thought about you hiding on the balcony in your wedding dress." He shook his head. "However irrational your actions, I'm glad you got out in the end."

"I am, too. I'll be right back." She jogged upstairs and used the light from her phone to look around Jimmy's office. If Adam were safe somewhere, she'd be able to put this entire ugly chapter of her life behind her—and move on to the next ugly chapter.

She opened the top drawer of his desk, using her blouse to cover her fingers. The tokens from Las Moscas were still there. The cartel didn't care if the police knew Jimmy had been one of theirs. Even better for them to warn others in their employ not to cross them.

Her gaze swept his desk. Looked like Jimmy had already disposed of the framed picture he'd kept of the two of them. Good. It had all been a fake, anyway. A fake relationship with a fake person, a person Adam had done his best to mold after

Clay. Did Adam ever tell Jimmy why he wanted him to act a certain way, like certain things? He may have mentioned an ex-fiancé in her past, but Adam never would've told Jimmy that ex-fiancé was Border Patrol.

She blew out a sigh and turned on her heel. She didn't need a fake. She had the real thing now.

BACK IN APRIL'S APARTMENT, Clay studied his former fiancée's face. They'd returned to her place in hopes of being there for Adam. The danger to April in her apartment had disappeared with Jimmy's death. A lot of things had disappeared with Jimmy's death.

If only Adam would come traipsing back in here, a smile on his hapless face, another scheme cooking in his brain, April could be free. As long as her brother remained missing, she'd stay hooked into his drama.

She glanced up from her phone. "What?"

"No luck reaching Kenzie?"

She clicked the phone on the coffee table facedown. "I texted her."

"We could try the Albuquerque PD now. You could report your car as stolen. If Adam's in the car, he'll be found."

"And arrested for car theft."

Clay rolled his eyes. "You don't have to press charges."

"If Adam is safe and driving around in my car, he would call me and tell me what happened unless he's still worried about Jimmy. He wouldn't know about Jimmy yet...unless he was there and Las Moscas has their hands on him now."

"April, you could come up with about a hundred different theories about Adam right now and still be wrong. There's no telling what your brother is up to. Leave it for the police. If he gets arrested for drugs, it could be the best thing for him."

"You're saying I should leave Albuquerque...or not, and forget about Adam?"

Clay's pulse picked up pace. "I think you should definitely leave Albuquerque. The place doesn't seem to agree with you."

"I wish Kenzie would call me back."

Clay wedged a foot against the coffee table. "You're not going to wait around here for Kenzie, are you?"

"You think we should leave?"

"Let's spend the night here like we'd planned and leave tomorrow." He toed off one shoe. "You don't have to be in Albuquerque to talk to Kenzie...or Adam."

April placed her hands together as if in prayer. "I hope he's okay."

He didn't feel like talking about Adam anymore or speculating about what happened to him. The guy had dragged his sister into a mess, all because of some hunch about El Gringo Viejo and dreams of riches. April's parents had made sure all their possessions would go to April because they couldn't trust Adam, even back then. Of course, April had done her damnedest to share her money with her brother. Nobody could ever talk her out of her support for Adam. She'd been loyal to a fault… to Adam.

Clay pinched the knotted muscles in the back of his neck. "Do you mind if I take a shower?"

"Go ahead." She hopped up from the couch. "I'll get you a clean towel and make up the other bed, while I'm at it."

Clay's jaw hardened. She was as controlled as the day she left him. If she could ignore the sexual tension that had been simmering between them from the minute she showed up in Paradiso, he'd have to follow suit.

He'd explored every inch of this woman's body intimately; it seemed absurd for them to camp out in different beds. But she probably had the right idea. What good would one night of passion do them if she planned on packing up and leaving him again?

His mouth watered as he followed behind her gently undulating hips to the hallway. That one night of passion could do him a helluva lot of good, come to think of it.

She swung open the door to the hall closet, almost bashing him in the face. "Sorry. I didn't realize you were right behind me."

He held up his hands. "I was daydreaming."

Her gaze shifted to his face as she reached for a towel. She pressed it against his chest. "Here you go. You brought toiletries in your bag, right?"

"Yeah, toothbrush, floss, the works." He shook out the towel and backed up to the small bathroom where he hung it over a rack on the outside of the shower door.

April seemed stuck in the bathroom's entrance, and he squeezed past her. "Do you need to use the bathroom before I hop in? I'm just gonna get my bag from the living room."

"I'm not even going to brush my teeth right now. I know I have a few beers in the fridge if Adam didn't drink them. Want one when you get out?"

"Absolutely."

She followed him to the living room where he snagged his overnight bag.

"I won't be long."

"Take your time." She waved a hand at him.

He didn't want to take his time in the shower alone. He wanted to hurry and spend all his time with April before they parted company again— maybe for good this time.

Seeing her again had only drilled home the point that he needed to get on with his life. She hadn't offered any explanations for running out on their wedding, even though the heat still burned between them.

Sometimes he caught a look of regret and sadness in her blue eyes, but whatever feelings lurked in her soul they weren't strong enough to overcome whatever objections she'd had to their marriage. He had to respect that.

He scrubbed his body hard with a washcloth as if trying to wash April Hart out of his pores. If only a little soap and elbow grease could do the trick.

He dried off and pulled on a pair of gym shorts and a white T-shirt—the more covered up, the better. Maybe he'd luck out and she'd be sound asleep after the events of today.

Did she really think he'd killed Jimmy when she saw him over his body? Not that the idea of April being engaged to a scumbag like that didn't cause rage to boil in his veins. Adam and Jimmy must've really done a number on her—or she'd been so lost she wasn't thinking straight.

Lost because of him? That's how he'd felt without her—lost, half a man.

He shook his head and draped the towel over the rack to dry. He stepped out of the bathroom and dropped his bag inside the door of the spare bedroom, which she'd already neatly made up for him.

The TV hummed from the other room, and he poked his head around the corner. "Still awake?"

She twisted her head around while pausing the TV show. "I'm not tired. Are you? I think I still have adrenaline pumping through my body from finding Jimmy."

He strode toward her and dropped on the other end of the couch. "I'm sorry. You must've loved him once."

"Never." She tightened her lips. "It was all fake. All make-believe, and I think I knew it even before the wedding day and my eavesdropping."

"Why didn't you make a run for it before the big day?" He crossed his ankle over his bouncing knee. Would she shut him down?

She shrugged. "Didn't relish the idea of being a two-time loser."

"Yeah, much better to be married to a man you suspected of criminal activity." He rolled his eyes. "Do you have those beers?"

"Just waiting for you." She half rose, but he sprang to his feet.

"I'll get them."

Her refrigerator contained a few bottles of water, a few bottles of beer and an expired yogurt. Why would it be stocked? She'd left this place to get married. Had they planned a honeymoon? Probably Mexico for a surprise visit to the bride's father.

He twisted the caps off the beers and tossed them on the countertop with a clink. "Do you want a glass?"

"You know me better than that."

He knew her better than anyone—or he used to.

He walked back into the living room on bare feet and handed her one bottle. She'd changed from the black leggings she'd worn earlier into short, pink pajama bottoms and a white top with spaghetti straps.

He pointed at the husky puppies on her bottoms. "Those look like Denali."

"Why do you think I bought them?" She dropped her lashes and rubbed a thumb across a white dog printed on the material. "It reminded me of Denali and…"

Her voice died away in a whisper, and a knife

twisted in his gut, engulfing him in the same pain that came on every time he thought about April.

He dropped to his knees. "Why, April? Why'd you do it? Why'd you leave us?"

Her sparkling eyes flew to his face, color rushing into her cheeks.

Okay, that had been a cheap shot throwing Denali in there.

She folded her hands around the bottle. "Would you believe me if I told you I did it to protect you?"

Clay curled his hands around her calves. "This sounds like the old 'it's me, not you' excuse. In fact, that's the reason you gave me two years ago."

Leaning forward, she placed her hands on his shoulders. "Does it matter to you right now?"

Clay swallowed. Did it? To have this woman in his arms again, loving her, pleasing her, meant everything to him.

He closed his eyes. He'd just been telling himself to move on with his life. Making love with April was not a good step on that path.

She cupped his jaw with one hand. "I missed you so much, Clay."

His lids flew open, and he found himself almost nose-to-nose with the one woman he'd loved more than life itself.

It didn't matter why she left. It didn't matter that she'd made terrible choices since then. It didn't matter that she intended to leave him again once she found her brother.

He scooped a hand through her hair. This mattered. Only this.

He brought her in inches closer and angled his mouth across hers. Her warm, soft lips opened, and she invited him inside. His tongue explored her mouth, and she sighed against his kisses.

She dropped her hand to the neck of his T-shirt and hooked her fingers over the neckline, rubbing her knuckles along his collarbone. Opening her legs, she hooked them around his torso, almost coming off the couch and knocking him backward.

He steadied himself and planted a trail of kisses along her inner thigh. The dogs on her pajama bottoms wiggled, and he smiled against her flesh.

He tucked his hands beneath her derriere and hoisted her back up on the couch, following her up and pressing his body against hers.

His erection, strong and sure, poked at her through the thin material of their clothing.

She wedged her hands against his chest. "You're squishing me. Let's trade places."

In a single movement, he wrapped his hands around her waist, turned and lifted her, taking her place on the couch.

She straddled his hips and pressed a kiss against his mouth. "Much better."

Tugging the undershirt over her head, he said, "Much, much better."

He cupped one pert breast with his palm and teased her nipple with the tip of his tongue.

She gasped and threw back her head. "That's wicked good."

"I don't want the other one to suffer." He dipped his head and swirled his tongue around the other nipple while pinching the one he'd already tantalized to a rosy peak.

She rocked in his lap, chafing against his erection, driving him crazy with desire and need.

He'd always needed April. It had gone beyond love. She'd percolated in his blood for years like some kind of addiction. He could almost pity the poor bastards dependent on drugs because April was his drug.

"Why are you still wearing this?" She clawed at his T-shirt, dragging it up his chest.

He yanked it over his head, and she immediately pressed her bare skin against his. "I love this feeling."

Her soft breasts brushed against the flat planes of muscle across his chest, and he soaked in the sensation. He traced one knuckle over the beads of her spine and slipped his hands into her shorts, splaying his hands against the curve of her buttocks.

He growled in her ear. "I love *this* feeling."

She wriggled against his erection, driving him crazy, and then dipped her head to his chest and grazed one of his nipples with her teeth.

Leaning against the cushions, he tipped his head back and concentrated on a little water stain in the corner. "You're going to take your time, aren't you?

You're going to do all kinds of little things to my body to tease me."

"I have an ulterior motive." She shoved her hand down his shorts and grabbed the length of him. "I'm going to make you so hard you're gonna go all night. You're going to please me like only you know how."

He dug his fingers into the soft flesh of her derriere and flipped her on her back, stretching out beside her.

As she started to roll off the edge, he grabbed her. "I don't think this couch is big enough for what I want to do to you—all night long."

She pressed a finger against his lips. "Let's continue this romp in my boudoir."

"Romp." He scooped her up again and staggered to his feet. "I like the sound of that."

He ignored the alarm bells in his head, determined to get his fill of this woman once and for all—as if he could ever get enough of April Hart.

Clay took two steps away from the couch with April clinging to his body, and then nearly dropped her when he heard the handle of the front door rattle.

Her arms tightened around his neck, and he brushed her ear with his lips. "Shh."

The door handle twisted again, and April slid from his body, stumbling backward.

The lock clicked, and Clay lunged for his weapon on the kitchen counter. He shoved April behind him and said, "Get back. He's coming."

Chapter Twelve

April crouched to the floor and peered between his legs at the front door, now easing open.

Clay shouted, "Stop! I have a gun."

"Clay?" The door opened wider, and Adam stepped over the threshold, brushing his dishwater-blond hair from his eyes. "Don't shoot, man."

April blew out a breath and pulled her discarded camisole over her head before jumping to her feet and rushing her brother. She threw her arms around his neck, momentarily forgetting that he'd set her up to marry a drug dealer.

"Oh my God. I'm so glad to see you safe."

Adam patted her back. "I'm all right, but we need to get out of here."

"Why?" Clay shoved his weapon in the back of his waistband, his jaw a hard line.

April stepped back from Adam. Now Clay would really hate her brother. Adam had just interrupted their reunion sex.

Adam glanced at Clay and then shifted his blue eyes back to April. "What does he know?"

"He knows everything, of course, and I think we even know more than you do." April tugged on the hem of her camisole. Adam wouldn't even notice their state of undress, Clay in gym shorts with his shirt off and she in skimpy pj's. Adam didn't notice much if it didn't concern him.

"What are you talking about? What could you possibly know that I don't? Jimmy abducted me. He thinks I have something that belongs to him."

April opened her mouth, but Clay crossed the room and stepped between her and Adam. "If Jimmy snatched you, why are you here? How'd you get away from Jimmy?"

"He was distracted. The cops are looking for Gilbert and it led them to Jimmy." Adam hunched his thin shoulders. "Let's just say, Jimmy had other problems besides me."

"You can say that again." Clay crossed his arms over his bare chest. "Jimmy's dead."

Adam's eyes bugged out of his head. "That's impossible. The guy had me captive as late as this afternoon."

April said, "We saw him, Adam. Saw his dead body."

Adam smacked his hand against his forehead and jerked his head toward Clay. "Y-you didn't kill him, did you?"

"I did not kill him, and you're lucky I'm not gonna kill you, either." Clay leveled a finger at Adam. "You set up April with this lowlife, manipulated her into marrying him for your own selfish reasons, not giving a damn about her or her feelings."

April pressed a hand against her fluttering heart. Clay had always stood up for her, always would.

Adam backed up against the wall. "Jimmy wouldn't have hurt April. He just wanted an in with our father, one that I couldn't give him."

"Cut it, Adam." Clay sliced his hand through the air. "Your father is not El Gringo Viejo. Get that insane idea out of your head. And if you didn't think April was in danger being married to a man like that, you're as stupid as you've always been."

A mottled red suffused Adam's cheeks. "I didn't force her to marry him."

"I know how you operate. Don't try to pull anything over on me." Clay rolled his shoulders as if to gain control of his emotions. "Did you know Jimmy and his gang were double-crossing Las Moscas?"

Adam held out both hands. "Hey, I had no idea until he told me today. That's why Jimmy wanted that flash drive. It contains tunnel locations along the border for the cartel's drops. I'm telling you the same thing I told Jimmy. I don't have it. Do you think the cops killed Jimmy?"

April perched on the arm of the couch, wishing she and Clay were wrapped around each other again. "The cops are not going to kill a drug dealer and leave his body on the floor of his house…or anywhere else."

"That's where you found him?" Adam's skinny neck worked as he swallowed hard. "Las Moscas."

"That's what we're thinking." Clay strolled to the couch, the gun still tucked in the waistband of his shorts, and put his hand on April's shoulder. "It's over. Don't involve April in any of your crazy schemes again. Don't ask her to search for your father in Mexico or anywhere else. Or you're gonna have to answer to me. Got it?"

Adam's gaze darted between April and Clay. "Are you two back together?"

God, she wished.

Clay must've felt the stiffening of her body. He dropped his hand from her shoulder. "We don't have to be together for me to look out for April's interests."

"Okay, whatever, man. I'm done with this stuff. I just escaped with my life." He rubbed his arms and sauntered to the table behind the couch. "Did you happen to find my stash here?"

"Disposed of it." Clay widened his stance, as if Adam would dare to take on him and his muscles.

April gestured toward the kitchen. "What happened here, Adam? Kenzie called me in a panic and told me there was blood all over my place. We didn't exactly find blood all over, but we did find smears of it in the kitchen and droplets in the sink."

"Yeah, um, Jimmy attacked me here." Adam danced from foot to foot, already missing his fix. "Hit me on the head and hustled me out. He must've cleaned up my blood before he left."

Clay tapped the cheekbone beneath his eye. "Outside of that shiner you're gonna get, you look in remarkably good shape for just being abducted by an angry drug dealer."

"Yeah." Adam traced his fingertips around his eye socket. "He roughed me up. Blood must've come from my head wound."

"Where did he hold you?" Clay narrowed his eyes.

"I don't know, man. They put a hood over my head. Then they got some calls, had some discussions and then stuffed me in my car... I mean, your car, April, and dropped me off in the desert. They loosened my ties so that I could get out, but not before they took off. I knew there was trouble with the cops."

"You're lucky they didn't kill you." April tapped her head. "Do you need some ice or treatment for your head?"

Adam's hand darted to the back of his head and he shoved his fingers into his long hair. "No, it's okay."

Clay asked, his face still tight, "Did you ever convince them you didn't have that flash drive?"

"I don't think so. That's probably why they let me live. If they offed me, they'd lose that information. They figured they could always pick me up again if they wanted."

"I wonder why they didn't just tie you up and leave you while they dealt with the cops." Clay rubbed his knuckles along the edge of his jaw.

"How am I supposed to know? I didn't have a clue how that guy's mind operated."

"And yet you were willing to marry off your sister to him." Clay's hands curled into fists at his sides.

April hopped off the couch. "Did they say why the cops were looking for Gilbert?"

"I didn't get all of that." Adam tucked his hair behind one ear and made a wide berth around Clay on his way to the kitchen. "You got a beer?"

She shifted a glance to Clay and took a deep breath. "We *do* know."

Adam ducked his head in the fridge. "Why were the cops after Gil?"

Clay strode across the room and hunched over the counter. "The guy you set your sister up with sent two mules—women—into one of those Las Moscas tunnels, but they didn't make it. Las Moscas caught them, beheaded them and proceeded to leave their body parts around Paradiso."

"Damn." Adam took a long pull from his beer. "That's brutal."

"Do you remember Gilbert's girlfriend, Elena?" April came up behind Clay and put a hand on his back. His rage at Adam kept bubbling to the surface and she didn't want to clean up any more of her brother's blood from this kitchen.

"I remember." Adam held his hand about chest-high. "Cute little Latina chick with a tight little body."

"That cute little Latina chick doesn't have a head on her tight little body anymore." Clay smacked his hand on the counter.

Adam jumped, and the blood drained from his face. "Are you kidding? Gilbert sent his own girl-friend into the tunnel?"

April set him straight...in case he didn't already know. "His name isn't Gilbert. It's Jesus, and he and Elena have been quite the Bonnie and Clyde over the years. That's how the cops traced her to Gilbert."

"Unreal." Adam shook his shaggy head and gulped down some more beer.

Clay fell back on the stool at the counter, strad-dling it. "You wouldn't happen to know the older woman Elena was working with, do you? White, maybe in her forties."

Adam rolled his eyes toward the ceiling. "Doesn't ring a bell. Damn, can't believe they used women. Did they think Las Moscas wouldn't kill a female mule?"

Clay ground out, "They were wrong."

"Are you going to stay here, Adam?"

Clay kicked her foot.

"I'll leave you guys and stay at my place, now that I know it's safe."

"Why'd you come back here?" Clay stood up and grabbed his gun from the counter.

Adam's gaze tracked Clay's weapon into his hand. "Honestly, just to get my drugs. I didn't know you'd be here."

"I didn't mean this time. I meant why'd you come back here when you knew Jimmy was look-ing for you?"

"I knew it was empty. I figured he'd try my place first or Kenzie's, so I wasn't going to go back there. Just needed a quick place to crash."

"And get high." Clay jabbed his finger at Adam. "You need to get clean, get your act together. April's not going to be bailing you out anymore. She doesn't owe you a damned thing."

April pulled her bottom lip between her teeth. Of course she owed Adam. She owed him for being her parents' favorite. She owed him for inheriting all of their mother's assets. She owed him because he'd been the one to find Mom murdered on the kitchen floor while she'd been off at school enjoying herself.

"Kenzie's thinking about going into rehab. I might join her." Adam tossed his empty bottle in the trash. "This just might be rock bottom for me."

"Did you drive my car back? Where did you park that you didn't realize someone was here? Clay's truck is in my parking space."

"I didn't want to advertise my presence." Adam jerked a thumb over his shoulder. "I parked down the block. Can I take your car to Kenzie's? You can pick it up tomorrow morning, but I will need my allowance a little early."

"Allowance?" Clay's eyebrows snapped together.

April ran her hand along the corded muscles in Clay's forearm. "Take the car, and we'll pick it up tomorrow morning. Leave me Kenzie's address because I have no idea where she lives, and she hasn't been answering my calls to your phone."

"Good girl. She probably turned it off so Jimmy

couldn't track me." Adam pulled open a kitchen drawer and grabbed a pen and a sticky note. "I'll write her address here, and I'll leave the car on the street in front of her apartment building. You can pick it up tomorrow morning."

"That'll work." She peeled the sticky paper from Adam's proffered finger. "And Clay's right. The two of you need to get clean. Stop associating with people like Jimmy."

Adam formed his fingers into a gun and pointed it at her. "Got it. Think allowance."

April cranked her head around the apartment. "Do you have anything else here?"

"No, unless you were kidding about those drugs." Adam raised his eyebrows at Clay, who scowled at him.

"I guess that's it, then." Adam skirted the counter and pulled April into a one-armed hug. "Take care. Let me know if you want me to pack up this place and get you moved out."

"You, too." April's nose stung. She couldn't help it. Adam would always be her little brother, a little lost and confused from the start.

He backed out of the apartment, jingling the car keys. "I'll leave these tucked in the visor in case we're not home."

April called after him, "Be careful. Jimmy might be dead, but we don't know anything about the others or the guys who killed him."

Adam waved a hand behind him before slamming the door.

Clay turned toward her stiffly. "Allowance?"

"Don't blame me." She patted her chest. "That was a condition of Mom's will. I got everything, but I pay out an allowance to Adam from the money. It's a cash stipend so he can't blow it all at once."

"He must love that you control the purse strings."

"He's used to it, but it's what fuels his get-rich-quick schemes or that's just genetic from Dad."

"Why are those schemes always illegal?"

"I don't know." She wrapped her arms around Clay's waist and rested her head against his broad chest. "I'm just glad he's safe—for now. And thanks for not ripping his head off."

"You could tell I wanted to?"

"And so could he." She caressed his face. "Let's go to bed."

Clay kissed the top of her head and then set her aside. He went to the front door and flicked the dead bolt at the top. "Too bad he didn't leave your keys."

"He'll need them if I have him empty out this place."

"If?" Clay slipped his hands behind his back and rested against the door.

"With Jimmy gone and his associates on the run, maybe I can settle in Albuquerque. It's not a bad place."

"Adam is here."

"For now."

"Do you think he's going to give up on his dreams of El Gringo Viejo?"

"Probably not."

Clay swore. "As long as he doesn't involve you, because if he goes traipsing down to Mexico asking the wrong questions of the wrong people, his encounter with Jimmy Verdugo is going to look like a picnic."

"I don't know." She plucked up the remote control and turned off the TV, which had been silently running in the background of their drama. "Maybe he learned his lesson."

Clay pushed off the door. "It didn't look like Jimmy taught him much of a lesson. Except for that redness around his eye, Adam didn't have any marks on his face for a guy who'd been beaten by a couple of thugs."

"He said Jimmy hit him on the head. That's probably where all the blood came from. Head wounds bleed a lot, right? That was enough to incapacitate Adam and allow Jimmy to take him away."

"Maybe." Clay covered his face with his hands and then dragged his fingers through his hair. "I'm sick of Adam and his problems. Promise me you won't fall prey to one of his scams again."

"Yeah, no, I'm on to him."

Clay drew close to her and brushed the pad of his thumb across the skin on her chest, right above her hammering heart. "You have a soft spot for Adam, and he knows it."

Standing on her tiptoes, she kissed Clay's irresistible lips. "I have a soft spot for you, Clay Archer."

He swept her up in his arms. "That's funny. I have something hard for you."

She halfheartedly pummeled his chest with her fists. "You have a one-track mind."

"Jimmy's dead. Adam's safe." He strode to her bedroom and kicked open the door. "What's stopping us now?"

THE FOLLOWING MORNING, April packed up again and went from room to room to make sure she wasn't leaving anything important behind.

As she cleared the bottles of water from the fridge, Clay entered the kitchen. "Are you going to leave those beers?"

"Might as well keep them here for Adam. It'll be his payment for closing up my apartment if I decide to leave Albuquerque." She shook out a plastic grocery bag and put a bottle of water inside. "Speaking of payments, I think I can find that guy's house again—the one with the car. Maybe I could even leave him my car as payment."

"I suppose you could do that if you're not attached to your car. The one you got from him is a junker."

"Mine is only slightly better, and I owe him for his trouble."

Clay touched her waist. "When are you going to stop feeling so guilty about everything? And when are you going to start spending some of the money from your mom? Why are you driving an old car when you can afford a new one?"

She balled up a fist and pressed it against her

midsection. "Would you be freely spending life insurance money you got from your mom's murder?"

"Your mom had the policy and named you beneficiary. However she died, she wanted you to benefit from it. That's how life insurance works. Look at my mother. After my dad died, she didn't hesitate to use his life insurance money to enjoy her life. It's what he would've wanted."

"Your father wasn't murdered." She tossed another plastic bottle into the bag.

"A car accident isn't much prettier."

Rubbing Clay's back, she said, "Your dad was a great guy. I miss him."

"But not my mom."

"Your mom never liked me, so it was hard for me to warm up to her." She lifted the bag and swung it from her fingertips. "She must positively hate me now."

"She's on a cruise somewhere in the Caribbean. I don't think she hates anyone right now." He snatched the bag from her hand. "I'll put a couple of these in the front for the trip, or one…you can take the other in your car when we pick it up from Kenzie's place. You can follow me. I'll keep you in my rearview."

"You don't have to worry anymore, Clay."

"What are you going to say if Detective Espinoza finds out you were engaged to Jimmy and questions you?"

"Tell him the truth. I was engaged to Jimmy, didn't know his line of business, left him when I had my suspicions."

"And if he asks you about Gilbert? He showed us his picture when he was Jesus."

She shrugged. "I never saw Gilbert or Jesus or Elena or any of them."

"You'd be lying."

"Sometimes you have to tell lies that don't hurt anyone if those lies protect other people." She grabbed her purse and hitched it over her shoulder. "Let's get out of here."

As she locked the dead bolt from the outside, Clay clicked his tongue and said, "Keep telling yourself that, April."

When they reached Kenzie's block, April spotted her blue compact across the street from her apartment complex. "There's my car. At least he followed through with something."

"Does Adam have a car, or does he always use yours or Kenzie's?" Clay glanced over his shoulder as he parallel-parked his truck three cars down from hers.

"He has a motorcycle." She threw open the door of the truck and stepped onto the curb. "Now let's see if he followed through with the keys."

Clay slammed his door and locked the truck with a beep. "Are you gonna go up even if he did?"

"No. By leaving me the car keys, I think he made it clear he didn't need to see me before I left town."

April held her breath as she stalked up to the car. She pulled the door handle and released a sigh. "It's open."

She ducked into the car and flipped down the

visor. Her key chain, with the big red *A* for the University of Arizona, slid down and she caught it.

Jingling the key chain at Clay, she said, "He actually followed through."

"Give the guy a medal." Clay smacked the top of the car. "Pop the trunk."

She straightened up and folded her arms on top of the open car door. "You don't need to put my bags in the trunk. I told you, I plan to leave this car with Ryan in exchange for the other one."

"I know that. Adam said Jimmy loaded him in the trunk of this car after holding him and dropped him off in the desert." He pounded a fist on the trunk. "Humor me."

Cocking her head to one side, April pressed the button on the remote to open the trunk. It clicked and sprang up a few inches.

Clay pushed it up and bent forward, shoving his sunglasses on top of his head.

April joined him, bumping his hip with hers. "Find what you're looking for?"

"I don't know what I'm looking for." He reached into the trunk and pulled out a hand towel, shaking it out.

April sucked in a breath and stepped away from the bloodstained towel. "Well, there you have it. Jimmy must've stuffed a bleeding Adam into the trunk. I even recognize the towel as one of Jimmy's."

Clay jerked the towel by one corner so that it

danced in the air. "This is a towel from Jimmy's house?"

Wrinkling her nose, April pointed to the edge of the towel. "It's the same color as the towels in his guest bathroom downstairs and has the same raised pattern on the bottom."

"All right." Clay kept hold of the towel and shut the trunk.

"What are you going to do with it?"

"You can't leave a bloody towel in the trunk of a car you plan to give away."

"You have a point there." Avoiding the towel, she leaned in for a kiss.

They jumped apart as a voice called from above.

April twisted her head around and spied Adam waving from a second-story window. She lifted her hand. "I wonder if he wants us to come up."

Then Adam disappeared from the frame and closed the window.

"Guess not." Clay opened the car door for her. "I'll follow you over to this guy's place. Do you think it's safe?"

"They're a couple of young guys whose only violent tendencies probably come from the video games they play."

"Who got duped into trading a car for a worthless rock."

"I'm going to make good on that."

"You've never been the best judge of character, April." Clay shut the car door on her retort and strode back to his truck.

She bit her lip as she watched him in the rear-view mirror. The only character she'd ever accurately judged was his.

The drop-off with Ryan went smoother than expected. That might've had something to do with Clay's large and in-charge presence hanging over the negotiations.

She made things official by signing off on a transfer and then joined Clay in his truck.

They spent the hours-long ride back to Paradiso catching up, as before they'd been too busy discussing heads and headless bodies and Jimmy and Adam and mules. Jimmy's death had freed her, and she couldn't even feel sadness for the man he'd been when they first met—because he'd never been that man. That Jimmy had been Adam's creation—and she'd fallen so easily into his trap in her desire to push away the memories of Clay.

She turned her head to the side and drank in his strong profile. As if she could ever forget about Clay.

Maybe they had a chance now. Maybe the ugliness that had swirled around her after Dad murdered Mom and disappeared had taken a permanent hiatus, and she could start living the life she wanted.

Clay jerked his head to the side. "What?"

"Just contemplating my future." She stretched her arms in front of her, entwining her fingers.

"Our immediate future involves getting back to Meg's so that I can pick up Denali."

She adjusted her sunglasses as Clay headed west

on the turnoff for Paradiso. "I wonder if Meg and Kyle have gone on a date yet. He's not married, is he?"

"No. You think they hit it off?"

"Duh." She cracked open her window, preferring fresh air to AC. "I'm surprised they hadn't met before. Paradiso is hardly a bustling metropolis."

"I've never played matchmaker before—except maybe between you and Denali. Now, that was love at first sight."

She whispered, "I missed…that dog."

"He missed you." Clay's knuckles turned white as he gripped the steering wheel. "And he'll miss you again."

April pressed her lips together as a pulse beat in her throat. She'd have to play this by car. She had no right to spring random thoughts on Clay until she'd had a chance to examine all angles. Hell, maybe he didn't want her back, anyway.

Ten minutes later, they were rolling up to Meg's house. Clay parked his truck behind Meg's car in the driveway.

"Good, she's home."

"It *is* Saturday." April jerked her thumb over her shoulder. "What are you going to do with that bloody towel you found in my trunk?"

"I'm not sure yet, but don't tell anyone about it… including your brother."

Grabbing the door handle, she cocked her head. "I'm sure he already knows about it."

"Then there's no need to tell him we have it."

Clay raised his eyebrows before jumping out of the car.

She didn't blame him for being suspicious of Adam, but did he think he faked his own abduction?

Halfway up the walkway, the front door burst open and Denali bounded down the porch steps. He shot past Clay and danced and circled around her legs.

April laughed. "Good boy. You know who's gonna give you the treats."

"Some welcome home." Clay crouched down, and Denali barreled into his chest, licking his face. "That's more like it."

"He heard your truck and started going crazy." Meg stood on the threshold, framed by the door, propping the screen door open with her foot. "Everything go okay in New Mexico?"

"Just fine." April waved her hand in the air. "Everything okay here? No more body parts showing up, I hope."

"N-no, nothing quite like that." Meg crossed her arms.

Clay's head shot up. "Did the other woman's body turn up?"

"No." Meg turned toward the house. "It's probably nothing. I'll show you."

April poked Clay in the back as she followed him up the porch steps. When he twisted his head over his shoulder, she rolled her eyes.

Once inside, Clay tripped to a stop and April plowed into his back.

"Hey, Kyle. You checking up on the security system?"

Kyle raised his beer. "Something like that."

April nudged Clay's upper arm and he rubbed it as if she'd punched him. "Why do you keep poking and prodding at me?"

She winked and then turned to Meg, hovering by the kitchen counter. "What did you have to show me?"

Meg slid an envelope off the counter with two fingers and held it up. "This was stuck under my windshield wiper today. It has your name on it."

April caught her breath but forced a smile to her lips. "Mysterious. You didn't see who left it?"

"No. I was at the grocery store. My car was in the parking lot and it was there when I came out."

Under Meg's watchful eye, April inserted her thumb beneath the flap and ripped it open. She withdrew a single sheet of paper, and her blood ran cold in her veins.

Chapter Thirteen

Clay nodded as he responded to Kyle's question, but his heightened senses were focused on April, a white sheet of paper in one hand and an envelope crushed in the other.

He held up one finger to Kyle. "Excuse me a minute. What's that all about, April?"

She held up the paper in front of her face and flipped her hair over one shoulder. "Just a note from a friend... Carly. She heard I was in town, but didn't know how to reach me."

Meg fanned herself. "Whew. I'm glad that's all it was. Why didn't Carly just come to the house and see me or leave the note in the mailbox?"

"Not sure." April squinted at the letter, which Clay would give anything to see. "She doesn't go into it here. Probably just saw your car in the parking lot and decided to leave a note."

April folded the paper, creasing it with her thumb, and shoved it into the wrinkled envelope. Clay followed the path of the folded envelope from hand to front pocket as a muscle twitched at the corner of his mouth.

Maybe it was another communication from Adam. Maybe another scheme. He knew damned well it wasn't a note from Carly. And now he knew April would never stop lying to him.

"We've gotta get going." Clay scratched the top of Denali's head. "I'll bring your bags in, April."

"Oh, April's staying here?" Meg raised her brows, but Clay caught the quick glance she threw Kyle's way.

"Of course I'm staying here." April flung her arms out to her sides. "But don't mind me. I'm exhausted from that quick turnaround trip to New Mexico. I'm going to grab a snack, a glass of wine and head to my bedroom to fall asleep in front of the TV."

All smiles, Meg responded, "That sounds like a plan."

Clay turned on his heel and April called after him, "I can come with you to get my bags."

"I've got it. Find yourself that snack and let me have my dog back." He whistled and Denali trotted after him, giving April one last longing look. Clay refused to emulate his dog.

The only reason he'd want to be alone with April was to tackle her and grab that note, but if she wanted to continue lying to him, who was he to stand in her way?

He yanked her bags from the back and eyed the bloody towel in the corner. Two could play these games and have secrets.

Clay dropped April's bags just inside the door and held up a hand. "Have a good night, everyone, and thanks for watching Denali, Meg."

He knew April wouldn't try to stop him from leaving. She wanted him out of here as fast as he wanted to be out.

Despite Jimmy's death, or maybe because of it, Clay heaved a sigh at the thought of Kyle spending the night with Meg. He couldn't shake the feeling that April's trials and tribulations weren't behind her. Maybe they never would be as long as she kept her brother in her life, but she'd made that choice. She'd made a lot of choices he didn't agree with.

He punched the accelerator and the truck leaped forward, leaving Denali scrabbling for purchase on the seat beside him.

"Sorry, boy." He rubbed the dog under the chin. "Looks like April is getting ready to bolt again."

Denali whined, rolling one ice-blue eye at him.

"Don't look at me like that. I tried, but at least this time I'm not letting her get away without knowing the full truth."

After he arrived home and unpacked, Clay scanned through his contacts for the phone number of Duncan Brady, a buddy of his in forensics for the Pima County Sheriff's Department.

He placed his phone on the kitchen counter and put it on speaker, getting ready to leave Duncan a message on this Saturday night.

When Duncan answered on the third ring, Clay snatched up the phone. "I didn't expect you to be home."

Duncan snorted. "Did you forget Olivia and I had a baby a few months ago? I'm pretty sure we got your gift."

"I guess your Saturday nights are booked up, huh?"

"Baby swings, diapers, trying to catch a few winks during those rare times the baby conks out, still rubbing Olivia's feet—although I'm beginning to think that one's a scam." Duncan snorted again. "Must sound like hell to a single guy like you."

Clay squeezed his eyes closed. "Yeah, sounds rough."

"In fact, probably the only reason you're not out raising hell on a Saturday night is because of that mess you have going on down there. Two heads and one body. Female mules. Makes me sick." Duncan sucked in a breath. "Is that why you're calling? Need some help with that?"

"Unofficial help if you're offering."

"I owe you a few. I can't remember which one of us is due now, but I'll hit you up later." Duncan took a sip of something, probably a cocktail, before continuing. "What do you need?"

"Need you to run a couple of DNA tests on some blood." Clay glanced at the two plastic bags on the counter—one with blood taken from April's kitchen and the other with the towel taken from the trunk of her car. "Under the radar."

"This is outside of Detective Espinoza's investigation?"

"Congruent with. I'm not doing a runaround on Espinoza, but you know how it is with multi-agency investigations. Stuff that's important to you won't get a second look from the guy and agency in charge—and Espinoza is in charge."

"I can do it for you, Archer." A baby wailed in the background. "Duty calls. When can you bring me these samples?"

"You're still in Bisbee?"

"Same place. You wanna bring them by the house tomorrow?"

"If I'm not going to crash your baby party."

"Hey, it's a party every day around here. Best time for me is around noon. Can you make it?"

"I'll be there." Clay cleared his throat. "And congratulations, man."

Clay ended the call and spun his phone around on the counter. Duncan had been a hard partyer back in the day when Clay had been with April. Now Duncan was the family man, and Clay had no one.

Denali barked and pawed at his leg.

"Yeah, okay, I have you. But let's face it. Even you have more loyalty to April than you do to me." Leaning forward, he cuffed Denali's sharp ears with both hands and touched his nose to the dog's wet snout.

When his phone buzzed, Clay grabbed it. His heart bumped against his rib cage when he saw the call was from Meg.

"Everything okay?" He couldn't keep the edge out of his voice and Denali perked up his ears.

"I—I'm not sure, Clay." Meg's voice dropped to a whisper. "You know that note April got?"

"Yeah." Clay forced the word past his dry throat.

"I opened it."

"You stole it from April?" Great minds must've been thinking alike. "I hope you didn't have to tackle her."

"What? No. I opened it before I gave it to her, and then I resealed it. I'm sorry if that makes me nosy, but…it's April and she found two heads on two different days."

"So?" Clay licked his lips. "I'm guessing it wasn't from Carly. What did it say?"

"The note was weird, like in one of those kidnapping movies with the letters cut out of magazines."

The blood pulsed in his veins. "What did it say, Meg?"

"It said, 'Nothing has changed. Stay away from him.'"

AS THE LIGHT of day edged into the room through the gaps in the blinds, April felt beneath her pillow for the hundredth time since she'd stashed the envelope there. Sleep had eluded her all night.

Her fingers curled around a corner of the envelope and she dragged it out. She stared at the white oblong in the semidarkness.

Who was watching her? Who was torturing her? Had this malevolent presence been waiting for her to show up in Paradiso again? And why?

She knew nothing. She had no information to give Clay about anything. She hadn't even known Jimmy when she and Clay had been engaged. It couldn't be him or his associates.

Her father. Was Adam right? Was their father some big-time drug dealer who didn't want his daughter married to a Border Patrol agent?

She buried her face in the pillow. It didn't make any sense. But she knew it was no hoax.

The first time she'd received the warning, the week before her wedding, her tormenter had tampered with the brakes on Clay's truck to show her he could get to Clay when and where he wanted. Then he'd kidnapped Denali.

Clay had no idea these events were connected or had any greater meaning than a patch of bad luck—but she knew. The person threatening her made sure of that.

She could've told Clay. He would've assured her that he could protect himself and her, just like he always had. But what if he couldn't? What if some day out on the lonely border, working on his own, Clay met with violence? It would look so natural— a Border Patrol agent running into a bad guy and winding up dead. It did happen.

But she would know. She'd know that she brought that danger to Clay, and she wouldn't have been able to live with herself. So much better to hurt him once, hard and fast, and leave him to find someone else, someone less complicated, someone less…cursed.

She rubbed her stinging nose. She'd been so close to staying here with Clay and making a life with him. She'd been trying to create that with Jimmy when Adam had given her a Clay substitute in

Jimmy, but she'd known all along on some level that it was all a big lie. Nobody could ever replace Clay in her heart.

But this time, she planned to fight for him, fight for the life they deserved together, and if the puzzle started with her father, then she needed to go to the source.

By the time she dragged herself into the kitchen, the two new lovebirds were chirping at each other over breakfast.

Meg looked up from her omelet. "Kyle made me breakfast. Do you want some?"

Kyle held up his fork and circled it in the air. "I can whip up another omelet for you, April."

"Coffee's fine for me." She reached for a mug on the shelf and poured some coffee for herself. "How'd the security system work the past few days?"

"Perfect." Meg fluttered her lashes at Kyle. "I felt so safe."

"I don't think you'll be finding any more heads on your porch." Kyle entwined his fingers with Meg's.

"I certainly hope not." April smiled into her coffee cup as she took a sip. "Did Denali behave himself?"

"He's high energy. I took him to doggy daycare on Friday, so he could frolic while I was at work. I forgot to tell Clay, but I know he's used that place before." Meg traced a finger around the rim of her orange juice glass. "Have you heard from Clay this morning?"

"Why would I? After two days together, I'm sure he needs a break from me."

"Sure he does." Meg rolled her eyes. "What happened in New Mexico? Did you close up your apartment? See Adam?"

"Might be keeping my place there, and I did see Adam."

"Is he still a troublemaker?"

"He still has issues. Why wouldn't he?" April's cheeks warmed in Adam's defense.

"C'mon, April." Meg's gaze shifted to Kyle, busily scanning through his phone. "Adam was trouble before…it happened."

"I know that, but finding Mom didn't help matters." April tossed her coffee into the sink.

"Of course not. That's just unimaginable, but you survived it."

Did she? Did you ever survive a trauma like theirs? "Everyone deals differently."

Kyle held up his phone. "They found her."

"Who?" Meg reached across the table and dabbed a string of cheese from Kyle's chin.

April gripped the edge of the sink. "The second headless body?"

Kyle nodded. "In the pecan groves down from Clay's house."

April clenched her teeth. She'd been walking Denali out there the other day. Had the body been there then? Had Denali sensed it? Smelled it?

She eked out a breath between her teeth. "Hopefully, they can identify her and put both of these women to rest."

"They were mules, working for a cartel." Meg screwed up one side of her mouth. "I wouldn't waste too much pity on them."

Folding her arms and grabbing her upper arms, April said, "They were exploited, probably told their mission didn't hold any risks beyond getting arrested by Border Patrol."

"Some women are easily duped." Meg collected the dishes on the table. "Kyle and I are going to Tucson today. Do you have any plans?"

"Just some errands. Have fun." April left the newly minted couple goggling at each other over the table and returned to her bedroom to shower and get dressed.

She knew she wouldn't be contacting Clay today. Whatever this was, this threat over their heads, she had no intention of bringing it down on Clay. He had enough threats in his life with Las Moscas littering the town with body parts. But this time, she planned to track down the threat. If that meant traveling to Mexico to find El Gringo Viejo, that's what she'd do—and she'd need Adam to do it.

When she got out of the shower, she glanced at her phone. Clay hadn't contacted her yet. He'd been suspicious about the note. Maybe his suspicions would steer him away from her for now.

She texted Adam to let him know she was ready to look for Dad—wherever that led them.

She hadn't been lying to Meg about errands. She had to get that car in her name, get some money, make some inquiries...avoid Clay.

By the time she left, Meg and Kyle were gone. April locked up the house and walked out to the car that almost officially belonged to her. She couldn't afford to run down to Mexico in a stolen car.

She took care of most of her business and decided to get some lunch before the next round. She ducked into the air-conditioned confines of a small café at the end of the main street and ordered a sandwich.

While she waited, she cradled her phone in her hand. Nothing yet from Adam and nothing from Clay. She must've sent Clay the keep-away message last night loud and clear.

She flattened her hand against her chest, over her aching heart. She'd come back to Clay one day— free and unencumbered by the dark cloud that hung over her head.

When she heard her order number, she picked up her sandwich, refilling her soda on the way back to her table. She stumbled and her drink sloshed over the side of her cup when she saw a man sitting at her table, his large frame spilling over the sides of the chair.

She hadn't left her purse there, but she'd left some napkins and the lid to her cup.

She cleared her throat as she approached the table. "Excuse me, but I was sitting here."

The man spread his fleshy lips in what looked

like an attempt at a smile. "I know that, April. That's why I'm sitting here."

She swallowed, her grip tightening on the paper cup in her hand. "Who are you?"

"Have a seat, and I'll tell you all about it." He pushed out the chair across from him with his foot, and it scraped across the floor, setting her teeth on edge.

She almost dropped her plate as she set it on the table. Sinking to the chair, she held on to her drink like a security blanket, all her nerve endings on high alert. "What do you want?"

He hunched forward, his double chin tripling. "I think you know what we want…Mrs. Jimmy Verdugo."

The drink in her hand jerked, spilling onto the table. "I'm not… I didn't…"

He held up his hand, his sausage-like fingers encircled with several glittering rings. "I know you ditched the wedding at the last minute—smart move. But we know you have Jimmy's flash drive, or your brother has it."

"I don't have it. I never saw it."

"If you don't have it, your brother does." He lifted the loose shirt he wore over his large frame to reveal a gun strapped to his body. "And you're gonna get it and him for us…or what happened to those two mules is gonna look like a garden party."

Chapter Fourteen

Clay's adrenaline spiked when he saw the big man who'd entered the café seconds before sit at the table April had been occupying. He dropped his binoculars on the seat beside him and charged out of the car. He burst into the restaurant and several people, including April and her tablemate, glanced up at him. He ate up the space between him and April in two long strides.

"Is this man bothering you?"

April shook her head, her pale face belying her response.

The man scooted back his chair and rose to his feet, patting his belly. "Just taking a load off. It's hard for a man my size to wait on his feet."

Clay's eyes narrowed. He didn't have any right to arrest this man or question him if April didn't open her mouth.

He put a hand on her shoulder. "Is that right, April?"

"H-he was just sitting for a minute." She'd pinned her gaze to the man's right hand, resting on his hip.

The man rapped his knuckles on the table. "You have a good day now, miss."

He walked out of the café with more grace than expected from a man carrying that extra weight.

When the door whooshed shut, Clay took the seat across from April that the man had vacated. "What was that all about?"

April picked up her grilled cheese sandwich and nipped a bite off the corner. She dabbed some crumbs from her lips, and then took a sip of her soda. Then she dusted off her fingertips over her plate.

Finally, she raised her eyes to his. "He just threatened me over that flash drive."

Clay jumped from his chair, knocking it to the floor with a bang.

As he took a step toward the door, April grabbed his hand. "He's gone. I made sure of that before I told you, so you wouldn't get killed."

"Why are you telling me this now when it's too late?" He shook off her hand. "I could've arrested him."

"He would've killed you." She lifted her shoulders. "He had a gun. When you were at the table, his hand was hovering over his weapon. If you'd made a move, he would've shot you."

Clay righted the chair and waved at the guy manning the counter. When he sat down, he scooted in close, almost touching his nose to April's. "I'm a Border Patrol agent. It's not your job to protect me. It's your job to report crimes or threats and let the authorities, including me, take action."

"I couldn't have warned you about the gun. I have no doubt in my mind he would've drawn on you and shot you—and then probably abducted me in the process." She waved her arm around the room of regular people enjoying their lunches. "Do you think any one of these people would've done anything to stop him?"

"You don't have much faith in my abilities, do you?" He raised his brows and took a gulp from her cup.

"When it's a fair fight I do, but not when it's a sneak attack or ambush. Anybody can get to anybody else if they really want to."

Clay smacked his hand against his forehead. "I'm not your brother, April. You don't have to look out for me."

"Speaking of my brother, he wanted Adam." She ripped the crust from her sandwich. "It's the flash drive again. He thinks Adam or I have it."

"Damn it." Clay pounded his fist on the table. "When is this going to end? Adam must have the flash drive, and I'm gonna get it from him."

"He said he didn't…"

Clay skewered her with a look and she trailed off, too embarrassed to continue.

"Exactly. We can't trust anything Adam says… about anything. He's probably had it all this time. Who knows if Jimmy and his guys would've been able to get it out of him, if they hadn't been distracted by their other troubles? I wish they had, and then when Las Moscas came to call on Jimmy, they would've gotten the flash drive from him and this would be over."

"And Adam would be dead."

"He's dead, anyway, April, unless he turns over that flash drive to Las Moscas. Do you think the fat man is fooling around? But now, Adam has dragged you into it—just like he always does."

"Maybe I can convince Adam to give it up. If it does contain a map of Las Moscas' border tunnels, Adam doesn't have the connections to make use of that information, anyway."

Clay spread his hands on the table, his thumbs touching. "Was this the note? Did this guy leave you a note to meet with him?"

April blinked several times in rapid succession. "Yes. I thought he was going to give me some information about why the heads were left on our porches."

"Do you have the note on you? Can I see it?"

"I burned it." She picked up her ragged sandwich and took a big bite.

"I could've taken prints from it." He cocked his head. "How did he know Meg's car?"

"He was probably watching the house before." She dug her elbows into the table and rested her chin on her palm. "How'd you know I was in this café? How'd you know to come charging in here? You always seem to know exactly where I am."

"Paradiso's a small town. I was driving out this way and saw your car parked on the street—just like before. I was coming in to join you for lunch

when I saw that goon at your table." He could lie
with the best of them.

"So join me for lunch." She glanced over her
shoulder. "In case he comes back."

"You told him you didn't have the flash drive?"

"Of course I did." She toyed with her straw, scat-
tering drops of liquid across the table. "I don't know
whether or not he believed me, but if I don't have
it, he thinks Adam does."

"I'm with him there. Any way you can talk Adam
into giving it up? To spare both of you?" He grabbed
her drink before she sprinkled it all over the table,
and chugged it back so fast the carbonation brought
tears to his eyes. "Scratch that. He's the one who
set you up with a dangerous man in the first place."

"I can try to talk to him. I may have a way to
convince him." She lowered her lashes, which told
him she had no intention of telling him what she
could use to persuade her brother to give up the
flash drive.

At this point, he didn't care as long as it didn't
involve marrying another drug dealer—or marrying
anyone at all. He drilled his fist into his other palm.
"How about some good old-fashioned violence?"

She flattened her lips into a thin line. "You pro-
pose to beat Adam until he tells you where the flash
drive is? Yeah, that's not going to work, and if you
don't think Adam would press charges against you,
you don't know Adam. He'd see that as an opportunity for a lawsuit and some easy money."

Clay curled his hand around his clenched fist.

"You're right. I don't know Adam that well. I'd always seen him as trouble, but more of a hapless, sweet screwup. But setting you up with Jimmy Verdugo?" He skimmed a hand across the top of his head, his short hair tickling his palm. "That's a low I didn't think he had in him."

"I didn't, either." April pushed away her plate. "I'm going to text him and tell him what happened here. I'm going to convince him to turn over the flash drive to you."

"Even if he does that, April, he's still in danger from Las Moscas. He may no longer have the info they don't want him to have, but turning it over to us isn't going to endear him to the cartel. They'll want their revenge. He's gotten into some real trouble—and dragged you with him."

"And I'm going to get us out of it." She held up a hand, palm facing outward. "Don't ask. Don't try to stop me. I know what I'm doing."

"When it comes to your brother, I doubt that." He placed his palm against hers and clasped her hand. "But you do what you have to do."

And he'd do what he had to do. He'd already dropped off the blood samples to Duncan. Two could play this game. Could he help it if she were so much better at it than he was?

April had two different sandals on in front of the mirror as she turned this way and that.

Meg and Kyle had convinced her and Clay to

come out to dinner, although neither one of them was in a festive mood.

After lunch this afternoon, Clay had shut down on her, and for the first time since she met him, she felt as if he had more secrets than she did.

The rotund cartel member who'd threatened her in The Melt hadn't left that note. Now she had danger coming at her from two different fronts.

Or were they different?

Had Las Moscas been behind the warning delivered to her two years ago about marrying Clay? Adam could've already been involved with Jimmy and Las Moscas at that time and maybe his new associates didn't want Adam to have a brother-in-law working for Border Patrol.

She covered her mouth, meeting her own eyes in the mirror as a little shiver rippled down her spine. Perhaps Adam had told Jimmy about his sister and his father, El Gringo Viejo, a long time ago and Jimmy had already determined the best way to get to the drug supplier down south was to marry his daughter, and to do that, she'd have to be single and available for his courtship.

She dropped to the edge of the bed and toed off the flat sandal in favor of the one with the low heel.

Adam had finally answered her text and agreed to fly out to Phoenix to meet her tomorrow. She planned to get to the bottom of this…and offer him her deal. All without Clay's knowledge, of course. He'd try to stop her and she couldn't allow that.

Meg tapped on her open door. "Oh, that's a pretty

sundress. If you're wearing that for Clay, does that mean the two of you have patched things up?"

"Patched things up?" April rose and flicked the skirt of the dress. "We didn't have anything to patch up. We're fine...as friends."

"Some friend. He sure seemed like he couldn't get out of here fast enough last night. Picked up Denali and—" Meg whistled "—out of here."

"We were both tired, Meg."

"Blah, blah, blah." Meg squared her shoulders in the doorway. "What's the real reason you ran out on the wedding? What was the excuse you gave Clay? 'It's me, not you?' 'You're too good for me?'"

"Ugh." April covered her eyes. "I don't want to talk about it, please. Can we just have a pleasant dinner without bringing up body parts or weddings?"

"Yeah, because both of those are equally horrific." Meg rolled her eyes. "Kyle and I intend to have more than a pleasant dinner, despite you two."

"It's not too late to disinvite us." April yanked a light sweater from the bed in case of overactive AC in the restaurant.

"Oh, no. You're not getting out of it that easily."

April breezed past her cousin and tugged on one chocolate-brown lock of hair. "When you're in love, you want the whole world to be in love."

A half hour later, the four of them were seated on the outdoor patio of Sinbad's, a Mediterranean restaurant in the center of town.

If she were on edge, searching for the distinct

outline of the man who'd threatened her today, Clay matched her in jumpiness.

She knew he had his weapon on his person. He always carried off-duty. Kyle was probably packing, as well. The big man would be a fool to make a move in a public place with two armed men at the table.

So, when would he make his move? Would he wait for her to come up with the flash drive…or else? And then what? Clay seemed to believe neither she nor Adam would be out of danger even if they no longer had the flash drive.

Of course, if her plan worked and Adam gave her the flash drive, the two of them would be long gone after she turned it over to Clay, anyway.

When they placed their orders, April swirled her wine in her glass and said, "Have the authorities identified the other body?"

Kyle groaned. "Are you really going there? Now?"

"You need more wine." Meg grabbed the bottle of chardonnay from the bucket and attempted to top off April's glass.

"I've barely had two sips of this." April placed her hand over her glass. "It was just a question. One question."

"Answer her." Meg tipped her glass toward Clay. "And then that's it. No more of this talk."

"The short answer is no."

Meg did a karate chop with her hand in the middle of the table. "Let's keep it to the short answer."

As Meg and Kyle relived their idyllic day in Tucson, April scooted her chair closer to Clay's and dipped her head. "What's the long answer?"

"They took her prints, but there's no match in the database. They'll start looking at some missing persons. She could be up from Mexico."

"But she wasn't Latina?"

"A lot of gringos live south of the border." Clay shrugged. "How are you doing after your encounter this afternoon?"

"I'm okay. Just wondering when the other shoe is going to drop. How long is this guy going to give me to convince Adam to turn over the flash drive before he takes action?"

"You should be far, far away from here when he decides it's time. Do your best with Adam and then go into hiding. Leave the country if you have to. You still have plenty of money." Clay encircled her wrist with his fingers. "Start spending it to protect yourself."

"I've been texting with Adam. I think he's close to at least admitting he has the flash drive."

"I didn't tell you, but Detective Espinoza didn't find Jesus, the man formerly known as Gilbert, in Albuquerque." He pinged his wineglass with his fingernail. "But he did find Jimmy's dead body."

"Imagine that. Does he concur that Las Moscas can take credit for that one?"

"He thought it strange, as did I, that Las Moscas would use a knife to kill a rival instead of a gun with a silencer to the back of the head." Clay put a finger to his lips as the waiter approached the table with their food.

Everyone got busy with their food, and Meg aimed her skewer from her kebab at April and Clay, waving it back and forth between the two of them. "I'm sure your conversation is not fit for polite society, but at least you're talking again."

"Meg—" April dragged a piece of pita bread through the hummus on her plate "—please mind your own business."

"I second that." Kyle pinched Meg's chin between his fingers and placed a kiss on her lips.

Meg and Kyle's infatuation for each other left April and Clay free to discuss their morbid topic. The more April picked Clay's brain about what he believed happened in New Mexico, the better prepared she'd be to do her own search. That search might go easier with Clay by her side, but he'd never agree to it and she'd already been warned about keeping away from him.

April's eyes darted around the patio strung with lights. Could her tormenter be watching them right now?

By the end of the meal, April and Clay had abandoned their speculations and joined Meg and Kyle in more pleasant conversation. Meg had a glow about her that twisted a knife in April's gut.

She couldn't be happier for her cousin, but she missed that giddy feeling of uncomplicated love. She and Clay had that once. Or had they? Had her life ever been uncomplicated since the murder of her mother and the accusations against her father?

Clay had been here at the time of the murder, a brand-new Border Patrol agent. She'd been away at school and they didn't start dating until she'd come back to Paradiso after the murder and after she'd graduated from college. The events swirling around her family had already tainted her by the time she met Clay, already changed her.

She'd been carefree, majoring in dance choreography, the world wide open. When she returned to school, she'd changed her major to accounting. She'd wanted stability, security, order. She'd been determined to take care of Adam, who'd gone into a treatment facility immediately after the murder.

Maybe that's why she fell for Clay. He'd represented stability and security to her.

And then Adam had stripped that away from her, bit by bit. Her brother's catastrophes had become hers.

Their dinner wrapped up with the two guys fighting over the bill until Meg plucked it from their dueling fingers and waved it and her card in the air for the waiter. "This was my party, and I'll pay for it."

Kyle bundled a tipsy Meg into his car and winked at April. "We'll leave you two the house. I'm going to take Meg back to my place."

As Kyle roared off, April raised her eyebrows at Clay. "Kinda pushy, isn't he?"

"Are you okay at the house by yourself with the security system in place?"

"Of course." April gave silent thanks to the dark desert night that hid her hot cheeks.

Clay was making it easy on her to stay away from him. She wouldn't have to convince him to drop her off tonight. She wanted an early start for Phoenix tomorrow morning before Clay could even realize she'd left.

"I have my gun, too. I'll be fine."

Clay opened the door of his truck for her. "Are you going to try to talk to Adam tomorrow?"

"Yes." She pulled the door from him and slammed it. Clay hadn't asked if that conversation was going to take place face-to-face—and she wasn't telling. She'd take that two-hour drive up to Phoenix and meet Adam's plane. Then she'd present him with her proposition.

Clay aimed his truck out of town, back toward her house. The wine and the meal had a somnolent effect on her, and her eyelids drooped as she leaned her head against the window.

Clay turned down the music on the country station playing on the radio and hummed off-key to the song.

April's lips curved into a smile. Clay had always been a lousy singer, but that never stopped him.

A loud noise reverberated in the truck, and April's head banged against the window as Clay jerked the steering wheel.

Another crack came out of the night. The back

window shattered, raining glass down on her head. She squeezed her eyes closed and screamed.

The truck squealed and the back wheels fish-tailed on the road.

"What happened? What did you hit?" She peeled one eye open and focused on Clay's profile.

His jaw tensed. "I didn't hit a damned thing. Someone's shooting at us…and he just got my tire."

Chapter Fifteen

Clay wrestled with the steering wheel. It took all the strength he had to keep the truck on the asphalt—and he *had* to keep the truck on the asphalt.

If he swerved onto the shoulder, the truck could flip or skid out to a stop. They couldn't stop. Whoever shot at them wanted to disable the vehicle. Wanted them to be stranded in the desert.

Through his teeth, he ground out, "Call 911 now. We just passed mile marker 11, just before the pecan grove."

He heard April scramble for her phone as the truck rattled down the road, lurching to one side as the air escaped from his tire.

She spoke breathlessly into the phone, giving the details of their location, vehicle and situation.

Clay shifted his gaze to the rearview mirror and swore.

April ended the 911 call and cupped the phone between her hands. "What? What now?"

"I see lights behind us. The bastards are coming after us and our crippled truck."

"Go faster, Clay." April's fingernails dug into his thigh through the denim of his jeans.

"I'm afraid to go too much faster on that bum tire. We're riding on the rim now. The whole wheel could come off."

"If they catch up to us, they'll shoot out the other tire." She twisted around in her seat. "I can't see any lights, but then I think we went around a curve in the road."

"How fast will the highway patrol be here?"

"The 911 operator said they were on their way. Out here, who knows how fast that is?" She snapped her fingers. "Your weapon. Give me your weapon."

"You can't go shooting into the dark." He reached under his seat for his gun and pulled out the holster. "Be careful with that thing. It's a little heavier than yours."

The truck jumped and wobbled.

"The better to shoot someone with." April grabbed the gun with two hands. "Loaded?"

"What would be the point otherwise?" He pushed the barrel of the gun toward the windshield. "Only take a shot if the car comes up beside us."

"He may not have to come up beside us." She jerked her thumb over her shoulder. "If he comes up behind us and shoots out the other tire…or the driver, we're in trouble."

The truck bucked against his control and he smelled burning rubber. "C'mon, baby. Keep going."

"Only a few miles to your place, Clay." She smacked the dashboard. "We can make it."

"There has to be more than one person ambushing us. They gotta know I'll be armed, and they're prepared to take me on."

"Us. They're taking *us* on."

The truck protested, rattling and weaving the remaining miles to his house, but they made it and he hadn't seen a return of the headlights in the rearview. Of course, their attackers could've killed their lights and be rolling toward them right now under the cover of the velvety blackness of the desert.

He turned into his driveway in a hail of dust, grit and smoke. He held out his hand. "Give me the gun, gunslinger."

April turned the butt toward him. "Are we going to stay here and wait for them?"

"Are you nuts?" He snapped his door handle. "I'll come out first and cover you into the house. We lock the door, and wait for them behind it. Get down."

He slammed the door as April's head disappeared. Squinting down the road, he circled the car and opened the passenger door.

"Let's go." He took April's arm as she slid from the truck. He pushed her forward in a crouch and protected her body with his like a shell, curving over her, one arm extended behind him, his hand clutching his gun.

They stumbled up the porch, passing the spot where the pink hatbox had rested only a few days ago, and a hot rage thumped against Clay's temples. He'd kill any man who came for April.

When they reached the front door, red and blue

lights bathed the house and a highway patrol car squealed into his driveway behind the lopsided truck.

Clay shoved his weapon into the back of his waistband and raised his hand, blinking into the lights.

An officer eased out of the driver's seat, his flashlight already playing across the truck's rim. "You the ones who called 911?"

"We are." Clay pressed his keys into April's hands. "Open the door and turn on the floodlights for the driveway."

April pushed through the front door and flicked on the lights.

With the scene lit up, Clay took a step down the porch. "Someone back there at mile marker 11 shot out my back window and my left rear tire. I kept the truck on the road and made it home."

"Did they come after you?" The officer shoved his flashlight into the equipment belt hanging low on his hips.

The other patrol officer crouched next to the back wheel and whistled. "Looks like you made it just in time. This rim is destroyed."

Clay took another step forward. "Officer, I'm Clay Archer, Border Patrol. I have a weapon in my waistband."

The officer studying the wheel popped up. "I know you. Female mule's head was left on your porch. This porch."

"That's right." Clay felt April behind him,

breathing heavily. "You didn't see another car on the road?"

"We didn't, but it could've been hiding in the grove. We radioed for another car. They're doing a search now."

"Do you want to come inside to take a statement?" Clay tipped his head at the open door, April in the frame.

Denali had come to the door to investigate the commotion. He sniffed at the officers' heels when they came into the house and then sat beside April, who rested her hand on his head.

Apparently, the dog was a better protector than he was. He'd allowed them to get too close to April. Had they been hoping to take him out and kidnap her to force her deadbeat brother to turn over the flash drive?

Did they ever have the wrong guy. Clay had no doubt in his mind that Adam wouldn't turn over the drive to save his sister or anyone else—but they didn't know that.

Clay cleared his throat and answered the officers' questions, indicating that this latest incident had roots in the drug trade and the two dead mules.

He avoided talking about the flash drive because pointing the finger at Adam and getting the police involved wasn't going to help April.

He didn't give a damn about Adam at this point.

He and April took the authorities through the chain of events on the road and Clay allowed them in his truck to look for the bullet that had crashed through his back windshield.

They found it lodged in the dashboard, and the anger and stress gripped Clay by the back of the neck. That bullet could've found its way into April's head.

When the officers left and he and April stepped back into the house, Clay shut the door and wedged a hand against it. "I'm not letting you go home to stay there by yourself. You're going to stay here tonight."

"Gladly." She entwined her arms around his neck. "But I hope you have some beers in the fridge because I need something to take this edge off."

"I'm with you there." He made a detour to his laptop. "I'm going to check the security footage just to see if anyone's been creeping around my house."

"I'll get the beers." She disappeared into the kitchen and said, "There's one road to and from your house. They didn't even have to know where we were to wait for us."

"You're right, and everything looks quiet on the security cam."

She emerged from the kitchen, a bottle of beer in each hand. She thrust one at him. "Here you go. I don't like to drink alone."

He clinked the neck of his bottle with hers. "Here's to surviving close calls."

She pressed the bottle against her lips and tilted her head back. "That was some driving you did. If

I'd been at the wheel, I'm sure I would've flipped the truck."

"We should've been more careful. I should've predicted they'd try something."

"Why would you?" She tugged at his sleeve. "Let's sit."

"Why would I? Because that dude threatened you in broad daylight in public."

"That's just it. He approached me like we had a business meeting or something. Gave me a proposition to think over. If he'd wanted to abduct me, he could've come into that restaurant and stuck a gun in my ribs. I would've gone with him without hesitation."

He sank beside her on the couch and propped up one foot on the coffee table. "So what are you saying? This ambush wasn't initiated by the big guy with Las Moscas?"

"I don't know." Sighing, she placed her bottle on the table next to his foot. "Turn around. You're hunching your shoulders."

He twisted around, presenting his back to her. He couldn't deny that his shoulders ached with tension.

"You know what?" She snatched up her bottle and rose to her feet. "Bring your beer into the bedroom, and I'll give you a proper massage."

He jerked his eyebrows up and down. "I was hoping for an improper massage."

"That could be arranged." She batted her eyelashes. "Everything locked up?"

"Locked up, secured, surveilled, Denali on duty, cops patrolling and my weapon by my side."

She blew out a breath. "I might just be able to get a few hours of shut-eye."

"Not before my improper massage."

"Of course not."

He staggered to his feet and listed to the side. "Whoa. That beer hit me hard. Must be the contrast between the adrenaline rush and a depressant."

"Good. We both need to relax." She took his hand and led him into his bedroom.

He should resist the temptation of her invitation. She'd lied to him about that note from last night. He shouldn't get in any deeper with her until he got some straight answers from her.

She nudged him down to the bed and unbuttoned his shirt. She slipped it from his shoulders and pressed a kiss against the flesh of his upper arm.

She grabbed the beer he'd placed on the nightstand, and held it out to him. "Finish this and lie down on your stomach. I'll release those knots."

He downed the rest of the beer and stretched out on the bed, his lids so heavy he couldn't keep them open.

April kissed the back of his neck and trailed a hand along his spine. Then she dug her fingers into the bunched-up muscles at the base of his neck.

He reached around to stroke her thigh as she crouched beside him, but moving his arm took too much effort. His heavy limbs seemed to sink into the bed.

As he drifted off, he felt April's hair brush his face. Her lips caressed his ear as she whispered, "I love you."

A smile tugged at his lips, but he knew he was dreaming.

CLAY ROLLED OVER and ran his tongue around his dry mouth. He rubbed his eyes, and then flung out an arm to reach for April, his fingers skimming over her coarse hair.

Jerking his hand back, he shifted onto his side and peered at Denali next to him in the bed.

"You're not April."

Without even opening his eyes, Denali flicked his tail twice and burrowed farther into the covers.

Clay dragged himself up against the headboard and massaged his temples. What the hell happened last night? He'd been melting under April's soothing hands one minute and comatose the next. He didn't even remember her crawling into bed next to him—he was sure he'd remember that.

He called out. "April?"

Denali whimpered beside him, but the rest of the house remained silent.

Clay rolled up in bed, disappointed that he was still wearing his jeans. Maybe that was a good thing. He'd sure hate like hell to have made love to April and not remember. Impossible.

He called her name again, and as the fog began to clear from his brain, his senses amped up and his nostrils flared. Did someone sneak in here and snatch her?

The sudden thought had his limbs jerking and he kicked aside the covers as he stormed out of the bedroom, Denali at his heels. His head cranked back and forth looking for April's purse, signs of a break-in...blood.

Instead of all those things, a single sheet of paper on the kitchen counter beckoned to him. He crossed the room and snatched it up, his eyes skimming the note April had left him.

She'd left early, didn't want to disturb him, had a lot to do today, blah, blah, blah. He crumpled the note in his fist.

She'd left to do something she didn't want him to know about. He slammed the balled-up paper on the counter and lunged for the beer bottle on the sink. He tipped the almost-full bottle back and forth and then emptied it into the sink.

He'd drained his own bottle. She'd made sure of that. He cranked on the faucet and slurped some water from his cupped hand. He swooshed it around his arid mouth and spit it into the sink.

He flung open a cupboard door and snatched a small bottle of sleep aid he used sometimes when the job got to be too much and he couldn't turn off the horror. He shook it, as if that could tell him if it were missing one or two tablets.

He didn't need to verify missing tablets to know what April had done. She'd had every intention of making her escape to God knows where with God knows who this morning, but had run into a detour last night with the shooting. So, she did the next best thing—slipped him a mickey so she could sneak out this morning without questions.

She knew there'd be no way he would allow her to go off on her own after the events of last night.

But what she hadn't counted on? He pulled his phone from the charger and brought up a GPS app. He could find out exactly where she was going— ever since he'd put that GPS tracking device on her car yesterday morning.

Chapter Sixteen

April glanced in her rearview mirror for the hundredth time since leaving Paradiso. With her gun resting on the seat beside her, she felt safe enough but she wanted to be ready in case someone came at her like last night. Because she didn't know who had ambushed her and Clay.

It could've been the big man from yesterday, making his move to kidnap her and force Adam to give up the flash drive. She snorted. As if that would ever happen.

Or it could've been her silent tormenter who'd seen her out with Clay and wanted to give her a little reminder of what would happen to Clay if she didn't stay away from him. Just like the reminder she'd gotten loud and clear two years ago when she'd called off the wedding to him.

Meeting Adam in Phoenix could kill two birds with one stone—she could get Las Moscas off her back by getting Adam to give them the flash drive and she could convince Adam to do that by helping him look for their father—and if he *were* this

Gringo Viejo character, maybe she could get to the bottom of this plan to keep her away from Clay. It all had to be connected in some way.

She loosened her death grip on the steering wheel. She'd hated tricking Clay, drugging him, but he'd never have allowed her to leave on her own. He'd understand someday.

She'd make him understand. Her explanation would go a lot further if she could also hand Clay that flash drive with the locations of Las Moscas' tunnels.

She'd left Tucson behind her about forty minutes ago, and barring any traffic jams going into the Phoenix Sky Harbor Airport, she should be there with time to spare before Adam's plane landed.

If Adam believed El Gringo Viejo could set him up in business, he might be willing to give up that flash drive. He didn't have the personnel to take over business from Las Moscas, like Jimmy did, even with a map to all their tunnels. He had to understand the foolishness of that plan.

She wished she could make Adam see the foolishness in all of it—using drugs, dealing drugs, being hooked into that whole lifestyle—but she'd never been able to talk any sense to Adam. Her brother hadn't been a bad kid, but he never viewed the world through the same lens of right and wrong as everyone else did.

Sometimes she felt as if she were the only person standing between him and total destruction.

If she let go, like Clay had wanted her to so many times, where would Adam be now? Prison? Dead?

She flexed her fingers. She couldn't allow that. He was the only family she had left. She owed him that. She'd tried to be the parent Adam had never had. For some reason, her parents never could seem to love Adam the same way they loved her. She never understood it, but when she tried to ask Mom about it, her mother had shut her down.

Forty-five minutes later, April rolled into the metropolitan Phoenix area, the shiny new buildings rising from the desert floor just like their city's namesake. Phoenix was Tucson's brasher, more modern cousin.

An hour early for Adam's flight from Albuquerque, April pulled into a short-term parking structure and swiped her debit card at the meter.

She located Adam's gate and took a seat with her strawberry-banana smoothie and a paperback snatched from the shelves at the souvenir shop—not that she needed to read a murder mystery at this point.

The book turned out to be the right choice, as delving into someone else's problems made hers seem almost tame in comparison. She jerked her head up from the book at the garbled announcement for Adam's flight. All she heard from the loudspeaker was Albuquerque, but that was good enough.

She shoved the book in her purse and pinned her gaze on the gate, now open for business.

She didn't realize she'd been holding her breath until she released it when Adam's shaggy blond head appeared among the disembarking passengers.

She raised her hand, but he'd already spotted her, a big grin splitting his face. At least someone found it easy to keep his spirits up.

She hugged him as his backpack slid down his arm and he patted her back. "Good to see you under better circumstances than last time."

"Are they better?" She cocked her head, taking in his new shiner. "I told you that goon from Las Moscas made contact with me in the middle of the day, and then someone was taking potshots at Clay's truck last night—almost killed us."

"But Clay saved the day." He hoisted his pack back onto his shoulders. "It's gonna be okay."

She touched the abrasion on his scruffy chin, which she'd missed before. "Have you recovered from your injuries already?"

"Kenzie's a good nurse."

"Do you have any idea if the detective from Pima County Sheriff's found Gilbert, formerly known as Jesus? As of yesterday, they hadn't."

"I don't have a clue. Nobody ever contacted me—sheriffs or drug dealers. I did see a few articles online about Jimmy's death." He lifted his narrow shoulders. "They chalked it up to the drug trade. Imagine that."

"Let's get out of here." She prodded his arm. "Do you have anything to pick up at baggage claim?"

He punched the pack on his back. "I have everything I need right here."

"I came early. My car's in the parking structure."

He ducked his head and tugged on a lock of her hair. "You've changed your mind, haven't you? You're going to help me look for Dad down in Mexico."

She whipped her head back, her hair slipping from his fingers. "How'd you know that?"

"You're my sister, April. I know you better than I know anyone."

She murmured under her breath, "I wish I could say the same about you."

When they got to her car, Adam tripped to a stop, his eyes narrowing. "What's this car?"

"It's my new ride." She knocked on the hood with her knuckles. "My new, old ride."

"Where's your other car?" He twisted his head around as if expecting to see it in the lot.

"I kind of did an exchange." She threw open the door to the back seat. "What does it matter?"

"I was kind of attached to that other car."

"Yeah, since you drove it more than I did." She grabbed the strap of his backpack and had a fleeting urge to take it and run off with it. If he had the flash drive in his pack, she could turn it over to Clay.

Adam wrenched the backpack out of her grasp and tossed it onto the seat. Then he slammed the door.

Oh, yeah, he had something in that backpack he didn't want her to see.

She noted the twenty minutes left on the meter—just enough time for her proposition.

With Adam in the passenger seat next to her, she rested her hands on top of the steering wheel. "I have a deal I want to make with you."

"I knew it wasn't going to be easy." He slumped in his seat. "What do you want?"

"I will go down to Mexico with you to search for Dad and El Gringo Viejo…but you need to give up that flash drive you stole from Jimmy." She crossed one finger over the other to form an X and held it in front of Adam's face. "Don't even try to tell me you don't have it. That's why Jimmy and his guys came after you. They know you have that flash drive—and now Las Moscas knows you have it. Give it to them, and you can start a new life with Dad, if you want. If he's who you say he is, he'll protect you."

After several seconds of quiet, April stole a look at Adam's sharp profile. He had his eyes closed and his hands in his lap.

Then he cranked his head to the side and his lips twisted into his boyish grin. "Sure, April. I'll give up the flash drive."

THE RED DOT on Clay's phone had stopped moving at the Sky Harbor Airport in Phoenix. His heart flip-flopped in his chest. If she'd gone there to take a flight somewhere, he'd never find her.

His foot pressed down on the accelerator of Meg's car. April's cousin had gladly given up her vehicle to him when she found out April had disappeared…again. Meg even did some sleuthing in April's bedroom and reported to Clay that her cousin had taken her suitcase that had been parked in the corner since she got back from Albuquerque.

Where the hell could she be going? Was she foolish enough to fly to Mexico and search for her father? At least that would get her out of the clutches of Las Moscas—on this side of the border, anyway. He knew they had operations on the other side of the border, as well.

As he drove north on the 10, he kept one eye on his phone. When the red dot started moving, he pounded his fists on the steering wheel. "Yes!"

As he barreled toward Phoenix, he watched April's location move from the airport to Tempe, near the university. The pounding urgency in his head didn't stop until that red dot did. With any luck she'd stay put.

He had the tracking device on her car, not in her purse, which would've been a much riskier proposition. If she parked her car and walked, he'd have to stake out the vehicle.

He was about thirty-five minutes out as long as April didn't move. Did she really think he'd allow her to disappear from his life again?

After a while, he sped through the traffic into the city and took the turnoff for Tempe. He turned up the sound on his phone so he could follow the directions to April's car. They led him to Mill Avenue, an area bustling with restaurants and shops.

As he cruised down the street, he had to hope

that he saw her before she saw him. Of course, Meg's silver compact was a lot less conspicuous than his white truck with the back windshield shot out.

The GPS directed him to make a right turn and he practically ran into April's car parked in the last spot at the curb. He crawled forward, looking for his own parking space. He made a U-turn and parked across and down the street from her car.

He drummed his thumbs on the steering wheel as he watched the pedestrians zigzag back and forth across the street. Should he get out and look for her in the many restaurants and coffeehouses or sit here and wait for her to return to her car?

She wouldn't be leaving her car in a place like this if she were taking off for somewhere else. She definitely planned to come back to the car—if she could.

What if this were the real meeting associated with that anonymous note? What if she were in danger right now?

The thought had him clutching at the door handle as a spike of adrenaline shot through him. He could at least try a little reconnaissance. He didn't want to put her in even more danger if her…associate? captor? tormentor?…saw him charging up to save the day.

He dragged his gun from under the passenger seat and shoved it into the holster beneath his loose-fitting shirt. The O.K. Corral was farther south in

Tombstone, but if he had to engage in a shoot-out to save April, he'd be ready.

He slipped from the car and looked both ways before jogging across the street. From the sidewalk, he hunched forward and cupped his hand above his eyes to peer into the car.

His gaze tripped over a sweatshirt bunched up on the back seat and he said, "Damn it."

He recognized that sweatshirt as Adam's.

She'd rushed up here to pick up her brother at the airport and was probably buying him break fast right now.

He banged the heel of his hand against the car window. Figured. He rubbed his hand against his thigh as he retreated to his car.

At least he didn't have to go rushing in to rescue her from Adam—he could wait until they got back to the car. Then he'd break up that little tête-à-tête, along with any harebrained and dangerous scheme Adam planned to drag April into.

He got back into the car and slumped in his seat, cradling his phone in his hand. He scanned through his messages and paused over the one from Duncan. He'd asked Duncan to put a rush on those samples, and he knew Duncan had contacts.

He tapped it. Duncan had gotten the results back on the blood samples and had some info for him in an email. Clay brought up his email and located the one from Duncan. He tapped it and downloaded the report Duncan had included.

He skimmed through it and enlarged the area

that contained the results. His fingers froze and he brought the phone closer to his face.

The blood in April's kitchen didn't belong to Adam. That blood belonged to a Jaime Hidalgo-Verdugo, whose corpse was found two days ago. It didn't take a crack detective to figure out that Hidalgo-Verdugo was really Jimmy Verdugo.

Clay's heart pounded in his chest as he scrolled down to the next set of results. The blood on the towel in April's trunk? That belonged to Jimmy also.

Dread pounded against his temples. It had all been a big lie—a hoax. Adam didn't have enough wounds on his body to produce that much blood. There was only one way Jimmy's blood could've wound up in April's kitchen and on a towel in her trunk.

Jimmy hadn't assaulted Adam. Adam had murdered Jimmy. Sweet, hapless Adam was a killer.

What did that make him capable of now?

Chapter Seventeen

April dragged the tines of her fork through the salsa on her plate next to her half-eaten omelet. Adam had agreed to turn the flash drive over to Clay after Adam located El Gringo Viejo, but April didn't trust him.

"Just give it over now, Adam. It belongs with Clay. Can you imagine what the Border Patrol could do with a map to the tunnels of Las Moscas?"

"Yeah." Adam downed his second cup of coffee and put his finger in the air for a refill even though his leg was already bouncing uncontrollably beneath the table. "They could do some serious damage to the drug traffic into this country."

"Exactly."

"Exactly." His blue eyes met hers over the rim of his coffee cup. He smiled, but the emotion didn't reach his eyes. It never did.

She'd always put that down to the drug use. How could you really feel anything if drugs altered your emotional state? But if she looked at the past honestly, Adam always did have a flat affect, even as a child.

"Adam, you don't have the infrastructure in place, like Jimmy did, to take over for Las Moscas. What good is that information going to do you?" She dropped her fork where it clattered against her plate. "I told you. I'll come with you to Mexico to help you find Dad. If he is El Gringo Viejo, you can start a new life down there with him. You don't need the flash drive for that."

"I give you the flash drive now for Agent Clay, and you bail on me." He held up his mug to the approaching waitress and nodded his thanks as the steaming brown liquid filled his cup. "Besides, if you found Dad would you really let him slide? He killed our mother, after all. You'd let him get away with that?"

She dropped her hands to her lap, folding them, her fingers twisting around each other tightly. "He's in Mexico. If he is El Gringo Viejo and the authorities haven't been able to get to him yet, why would they be able to get to him just because I dimed him off?"

Adam shrugged. "They probably wouldn't. But can you imagine what I could do with knowledge of Las Moscas' tunnels *and* backing from El Gringo Viejo?"

"That's not our deal." She wrapped her fist around her fork and stabbed her eggs. "What you *could* do? I thought you just wanted money in exchange for that flash drive. I thought you just wanted some protection from Dad. What are you planning?"

"Dream big, April." He shook out a packet of sugar and dumped it into his coffee. He stirred it so that it created a whirlpool in the liquid. Then he placed the spoon on the table with a hand not altogether steady.

She glanced sharply at his eyes, dilated and darting around the room. "Are you on something now?"

"Not at all." He rubbed his hands together. "I'm high on life. Isn't that what you always told me to be, April?"

"I don't understand why you need me to find Dad."

"You know why." He blew on the surface of his coffee and then slurped it up. "You were always their favorite. You could do no wrong in their eyes. Dad never paid much attention to me. Why would he want to see me now? But you?"

"He hasn't tried to contact me once since he disappeared."

"Because he thinks you think he killed Mom, but we know better, don't we? If we could somehow get word to him to let him know we don't believe in the setup, he'd want to see you in a heartbeat. C'mon, you want to find him, too, or you wouldn't be here."

April clasped the back of her neck and dug her fingers into her flesh. "I meant what I said about the flash drive, Adam. I want to turn that over to Clay."

"Clay, Clay, Clay." Adam smacked the table

three times with each utterance of Clay's name. "I thought you were over that guy."

"Over?" April sat up straight, lining up her back against the booth. "This doesn't have anything to do with my relationship with Clay. He's Border Patrol. Just when they think they have all the tunnels under surveillance, another one pops up. That flash drive could be tremendously helpful in their efforts to stop drug traffic across the border."

"What are you, a public service announcement?" Adam snorted and started picking potatoes off her plate.

"Adam, I had no idea you were looking to get into the drug trade yourself. I don't support that at all."

"But you support my working with Dad in the drug trade?"

She shoved her plate away. "You don't even know if Dad is El Gringo Viejo. This whole thing could be a wild-goose chase. Clay said…"

"Stop. Not interested in what Clay has to say." He tapped his knife against his plate. "Is that why you're agreeing to helping me find Dad? You don't believe we will find him or, if we do, he's not El Gringo Viejo and he'll take me off your hands. Then you'll be free of me, and you can spend all of Mom's money and sell her house and not give any to me."

April had heard this poor-me story many times before. This time it raised a flag of anger in her breast. If Adam had more self-control, Mom would've trusted him with money and a share of her home.

"My goal was never to help you become a drug dealer. You must know that or you wouldn't have had to trick me into marrying Jimmy."

"I didn't force you to marry him. You agreed to his proposal all by yourself."

"Because you modeled him into something and someone he wasn't. You took advantage of my vulnerable state. I can't believe you set me up, and I can't believe I fell for it."

She covered her eyes with one hand, but she didn't feel sad or broken. Anger had started percolating in her veins. Adam wouldn't even make this deal with her. She'd help him find Dad or maybe they wouldn't, but he'd never turn over the flash drive to her.

"Jimmy wasn't going to hurt you. He wanted access to El Gringo Viejo, just like I do. After you helped us, I'm sure Jimmy would've consented to a divorce or annulment." He slurped his coffee. "Probably would've paid you off, too."

"As if that's what I wanted." She dug some cash out of her purse. "But you must've decided to go it alone without Jimmy when you stole the flash drive. Why'd you do that?"

"Opportunity presented itself one day."

"Who thinks like that?" She smacked down her money for her half-eaten meal. "I'm done, Adam. If you won't give me the flash drive now, I'm not going to help you find Dad or El Gringo Viejo or any other gringo. I'll tell Clay that you have the flash drive with intel on Las Moscas, and the authorities will arrest you. Whether or not you can keep safe from Las Moscas in prison is going to be your concern. My concern will be staying alive, as you've seen fit to put my life in danger."

Throughout her tirade, Adam had shoved his hand into his backpack. Maybe she'd gotten through to him. Maybe he'd give her the flash drive now.

Instead, he dropped his hands into his lap, and his lips curled up into a smile. "You're not going to do any of that, April. You're going to help me, just like you always have to make up for our parents' treatment of me."

"I'm sorry for the way Mom and Dad treated you, but that's not my fault, either." She draped the strap of her purse across her body. "I'm going back to Paradiso."

"No, you're not. You're coming with me just like you promised. And if you don't? I'm going to shoot you with your own gun, which is pointing at you right now."

CLAY SHOT UP in his seat as April rounded the corner with Adam close by her side, holding her arm. Adam never displayed much affection, so April must've agreed to do his bidding. If so, he probably hadn't told her he was the one who'd killed Jimmy. Even April wouldn't condone that from Adam.

He gritted his teeth. He now had in his possession a surefire way to pry April away from her unhealthy codependence with her brother—and he planned to use it.

He threw open the car door and stepped into the street. Adam must've seen him immediately because his head jerked up and he moved behind April's car.

"Damn him." Clay jogged across the street, facing them down the sidewalk. As he moved rapidly toward them, April swiveled her head around and held out one hand.

Adam created some space between himself and April, and Clay lurched to a stop when he saw the gun jabbed into her side.

Clay's eyes darted to the pedestrians on the street behind Clay and April. Nobody could see a thing.

With his hand hovering over his holstered gun, Clay drew closer to the car. "Let her go, Adam. I know everything. I know you're the one who killed Jimmy. Jimmy's blood was all over, not yours."

April gasped and wrenched away from Adam.

Adam pinned her between his body and the passenger door of the car, the barrel of the gun still beneath her ribs. "Stay back, Archer, or I'll kill her, too."

"He means it, Clay. Let us go. I'll be okay."

Adam reached back and yanked April's hair. "You told him you were meeting me? You liar."

April opened her mouth, but Clay growled. "Of course she told me. She didn't trust you."

Adam snorted. "That's rich. She didn't trust you, either. That's why she never told you why she called off your wedding. Thing is, Archer, she was having a fling with Jimmy Verdugo while she was engaged to you."

"Clay." His name ended in a cry on April's lips as Adam yanked her hair again.

"We've got some business to attend to. So, back off or I'll shoot her right here, right now. You don't think I'd hurt family? Think again." Adam chuckled, and the hair on the back of Clay's neck quivered. "I did it before."

April sagged against the car, her mouth gaping open.

"Now, back off or I'll kill her and find my own way to my father. At least this way, once she helps me, I'll let her go. And don't send the cops after us because one hint of that and I'll off both of us."

Adam opened the door and forced April in ahead of him. He held the weapon on her as she crawled over the console into the driver's seat.

The only thing keeping Clay from charging Adam was that gun pointed at April…and the fact that he'd be able to track them wherever they went. Adam believed April had told Clay where she was going, and he wanted to make sure Adam was still under that impression. Did April realize he'd tracked her car through GPS?

He wanted to give her some sign, but he didn't want to reveal anything to her psycho brother— and he was a psycho. Had he really killed his own mother, as he'd implied?

Clay held his hands out to his sides. "If you harm

one hair on her head, I'll come after you, Adam. I don't care if you're in Mexico or Morocco. I'll find you."

Adam slammed the door and waved a hand out the window as April made a U-turn and rolled up to the intersection.

As he charged back to Meg's car, Clay brought up the GPS app. He'd have to stay far enough behind them so that Adam wouldn't catch a glimpse of him, but close enough so that he could help April if she needed it.

She needed it.

He got behind the wheel and gripped the top with both hands, ready to take off now. He had to take several deep breaths to keep still and not make any rash moves.

What Adam told him about April and Jimmy was a lie. Whatever April was, she wasn't a cheat. Adam had wanted him to turn on April, abandon her. That would never happen.

He'd follow April to the ends of the earth. And when he got her back—he'd kill her brother.

Chapter Eighteen

As they barreled through the Sonoran Desert hell-bent for the border, April licked her dry lips and flicked a glance at Adam, still pointing the gun at her. They'd barely said two words to each other on the ride from Phoenix. Too many thoughts had been jumbling around her brain for her to give voice to any of them—until now with the border looming ahead of them.

"What did you mean back in Phoenix about killing another family member?" A sob escaped her lips despite her best efforts. "Did you kill Mom?"

"C'mon, April. You never suspected?" He tucked a long strand of dirty-blond hair behind his ear. "You always saw what you wanted to see when you looked at me—the little brother in need of rescue."

"When I should've seen what?" She dropped her voice to a raspy whisper. "What Mom and Dad always saw?"

"That's right." He turned his blue eyes on her, more vacant than usual. "They were afraid, ashamed, to admit that I might have issues. So, they just shut me out and tried to punish the disturbed kid who liked to set fires and kill birds."

"The pecan grove by the Dillons' house?"

"Yeah, that was my handiwork." He took a swig of water from the bottle in the cup holder. "Old news."

"It's not old news to me. Why'd you murder Mom?"

"Money, mostly." He rolled his shoulders. "Of course, you got the big bucks, but I always figured I could get more out of you than Mom."

"And Dad? Why did he run if he didn't do it?" Her gaze dropped to the gun leveled at her midsection. Maybe if she kept Adam talking, the gun would slip and she could get away from him.

She scanned the vast, empty desert that stretched before them. She wouldn't be able to get away from Adam unless she killed him. "I actually admired Dad's get-rich-quick schemes, but he did wander into illegal territory. I was tracking his activities. I knew exactly what he was involved in—and I hate to shatter your illusions, but he was dabbling in the drug trade."

"That doesn't explain why he ran, why he took the rap for Mom's murder. He must've known he was a suspect."

"He did. The drug dealers who killed Mom made sure of it."

"You killed Mom. Why did Dad think drug dealers got to her?"

Adam flicked his fingers in the air. "I made him

think that. You may be the one with the college de-
gree in the family, but I was always smarter than
you, April. My IQ tested off the charts."

"Deviousness is not intelligence." She grabbed
her throat. "The threats. The threats I got regard-
ing Clay. That was you?"

"I couldn't have my own sister married to a Border Patrol agent. That would seriously put a crimp
in my activities. I had to keep you on my side. I
knew Archer could turn you against me."

"But you weren't in Paradiso the other day when
I got that note."

"I still have friends in Paradiso, very loyal
friends. This particular friend even followed you
home from dinner and shot out Archer's tire." He
chuckled with no humor. "Larissa always was a
good shot."

"Larissa? The waitress at the Paradise Café?"

"I told her to keep an eye on you two and let
me know if you were together. I knew it would
be trouble if you ran to Archer—and I was right."
Adam curled his leg and bashed his foot against
the glove box. "He found evidence in the trunk of
your car, didn't he? Evidence that he must've had
tested to prove Jimmy was the one bleeding and in
distress, not me."

"Clay was telling the truth? You murdered
Jimmy?"

"Hey." He patted his chest with his open palm. "I
thought you'd like that one. Jimmy never got physi-
cal with you, but he probably would have. He was

a scumbag. I would've saved you from him even if you hadn't figured out his true identity."

"Why?" She held out her hand. "Never mind. You killed him over the flash drive, didn't you?"

"The minute I saw the information on that flash drive, I knew I had to have it. It's my big break, just like Jimmy knew it was his big break." He hunched his shoulders. "One of us had to go."

Adam directed her off the highway, down a utility road, and April's gut twisted. He was going to force her across the border—probably through one of the tunnels Las Moscas detailed on the map.

Would Clay be able to find them? She knew as soon as Clay told Adam that she'd texted him with their location that he must've put some sort of tracking device on her car or in her purse. That's how he'd found them in Phoenix. That's why he'd risked letting her get in the car with Adam—not that he could've done much in that situation. The minute he pulled his gun, Adam would've shot her. She had no doubt in her mind that her brother was a stone-cold sociopath. He had no feelings for her other than a need to use her.

If Clay had planted the GPS device on the car, once they left the car he'd no longer be able to find them. As her gaze tracked over the desert landscape, she knew they were going to leave the car.

"If Dad knows what you are, why do you think he'll help you now?"

"As El Gringo Viejo, Dad has moved up in the world. I didn't know he had it in him. He'll understand now how much I can bring to his organization." Adam patted her hand on the steering wheel. "You'll help me find him, April. You'll help me, just like you always have."

His touch made her flesh crawl, but she tried not to jerk away from him. "I will help you, Adam. We'll look for Dad together, and then you have to let me go. You can stay down here and work with El Gringo Viejo. I'll go back to LA and forget all about this."

Adam twisted a strand of hair around his finger. "No, you won't. You'll go back to Archer, just like you always do."

"I won't. I swear I won't. It's over between us. H-he'd never take me back, anyway." She curled her hands around the steering wheel so tightly the car wobbled.

"Right. That guy would take you back even if *you* were the one who committed murder." He drove a finger into his chest. "Even someone like me who doesn't understand love can see that Archer will never let you go—but he has to. Do you understand me, April?"

"I do. I do. I'll go to LA." She swallowed a lump in her throat. "I did it before. If Clay's life is in danger, I'll never see him again."

Adam swept his finger from pointing at himself to pointing at her. "Don't forget that. If you don't forget that, everything will be fine. You might even want to stay with me and Dad. You could do his books with some creative accounting. It could be a family business."

April managed a weak smile as she nodded. "Maybe."

But she knew in her heart that Adam would kill her. Once she'd served her last purpose for him—finding their father—he'd get rid of her.

Adam pulled a piece of paper from his pocket and consulted it. "We're almost there."

Five minutes later of hard driving over a sand-swept utility road, Adam knocked his knuckles on the window. "Here. Pull the car over by that rock."

April parked where Adam directed her. "Is someone going to pick us up here?"

"Why would I need that?" He shook out the paper in his hand. "I have a map to a tunnel that'll get us right across the border. We'll have to walk some on the other side, but I've made arrangements. It's amazing what doors are opened for the daughter of El Gringo Viejo."

"It's hot. Do you have water?"

"I've taken care of everything. I only pretended to be an idiot to get your help." He winked. "I'm not really an idiot, April."

You're something worse.

"Open your door and get my backpack and sweatshirt from the back seat. Then start walking toward that cactus on the right. I'll be right behind you."

With her fingers resting on the keys in the ignition, she said, "You don't have to wave that gun at me anymore, Adam. Where would I go?"

"You're not going anywhere without me." He slapped her hand away from the ignition and yanked the keys out. "But if I don't have the gun, you could get your hands on the gun."

"I—I'd never hurt you, Adam."

He cocked his head and a lock of hair fell over one eye, like it used to when he was a kid. "Out of the car. No sudden moves."

She followed his instructions and studied the sand beneath her feet. Could she leave footprints for Clay to track her to the tunnel? The sand in the desert never stayed smooth. Animals, reptiles, birds, the wind, the rain…all had an impact on the environment, leaving indentations and imprints on the desert floor. One step in the sand might look like a footprint, but the dry, shifting winds could just as easily cover it up.

Clay would know the direction of the border, but how long would it take him to find the entrance to the tunnel? It's not like they had neon welcome signs at the entrance. But Clay was Border Patrol. He'd found his way into many tunnels along the border.

Adam scrambled out of the car, still keeping her at gunpoint. "Let's get moving. The tunnel is just about a five-minute walk."

In desperation and with her back to Adam, April yanked the double strand of beads from her neck and curled both fists around the smooth, wooden pellets.

If Clay couldn't follow their footprints, she'd

leave another kind of bread-crumb trail. She'd been protecting him all this time from her brother. Now she needed Clay's protection.

CLAY ZEROED IN on the stationary red dot on his phone's display. Thank God, they'd stopped moving. They'd stopped moving in the middle of the Sonoran Desert, just north of the border. Adam planned to cross through to Mexico from one of the cartel's tunnels.

Would he be able to discern Adam and April's direction once they left the car? And if Adam saw his car roaring up? He didn't have a choice. He could leave the car farther back, but he had to get close enough so that he could reach them before they went too far into Mexico.

As he rumbled along the access road, he noted just enough undulation in the landscape that he could keep the car out of sight.

He caught his breath when he saw April's car abandoned by a large rock. He pulled to the side of the road, and then made his call to Border Patrol. By the time the agents showed up, April wouldn't be under Adam's threat anymore.

He'd make sure of it.

He left his own car and made the trek to April's. When he got to the car, he gulped back some water and wiped his mouth with the back of his hand.

Nobody on the horizon. They must've already entered the tunnel. He estimated the location of the border, but the tunnel could be anywhere along there.

Trying to track footprints wouldn't do much good. He dropped his head and scanned the ground, an unrelenting sea of beige tones.

A darker pebble caught his attention and he strode forward and crouched down. He reached for the object and sucked in a breath when he cupped the blue-and-yellow painted wooden bead in his hand. April had been wearing this necklace—and now she was using it to show him the way.

APRIL DRAGGED IN lungfuls of fresh air as she staggered from the tunnel, blinking in the waning daylight. When Adam had pushed her through the entrance to the tunnel on the other side of the border, she'd expected crawling the half mile on her belly, warding off scorpions and desert rodents. Instead, she'd walked upright through a large space fortified with wood and swept clean of debris.

She had two seconds to herself before Adam joined her outside, the gun still clutched in his hand as it had been through their entire journey.

"What now?" She rubbed her arms with hands now empty of all the beads she'd deposited at the mouth of the tunnel on the US side of the border.

"We walk to a meeting place about a mile ahead. I arranged transportation for us to Rocky Point. We went there with Mom and Dad when we were kids. Remember?"

She nodded, blinking back tears. She remembered Mom trying to create some family memories that didn't include trying to manage Adam.

Once they walked away from this tunnel and got into a car, Clay wouldn't be able to find them. He wouldn't be able to save her.

She scuffed through the sand, away from the tunnel, and perched on the edge of a rock, wrapping her arms around her legs. "I need to rest before we undertake a mile hike through the desert."

"It's almost night." Adam spread his arms wide. "The sun will set shortly. We'll be fine."

"I want to wait until it goes down a little more. I'm kind of claustrophobic. Walking through that tunnel drained me."

He leaned against the outcropping that masked the tunnel's entrance, taking refuge in the shade of the scrubby bush that protruded from the rock—just where she wanted him. "Don't try anything stupid, April. There's nowhere for you to run, and once my associates get here there's not going to be anyplace for you to hide, either. Let's just find Dad, and then we'll figure things out."

Figure out how to kill her and get rid of her body.

"What if Dad isn't El Gringo Viejo? What then?"

"If he isn't, which I highly doubt, I still have the flash drive with the tunnels. With that information, I'm sure I can gather a team to help me take over business from Las Moscas."

"They'll kill you."

"They haven't yet." He rubbed a hand across the

246 of Evasive Action

dark blond stubble on his chin. "They've been easy to play."

"Play?" She rolled her eyes. "You've played Las Moscas? Like that big man who came to Paradiso to threaten my life—and yours?"

"Yes, play, as in directing their attention to Gilbert and the others in Jimmy's crew, while I took care of Jimmy."

"Gilbert and Jimmy's entourage are all dead?"

"Do you think I'm an amateur, April? Is that what you think? I've been playing these games for years—you just never wanted to see it. Your obtuseness came in handy, or—" he tapped his boot against the rock "—maybe it was a survival mechanism. Maybe you knew on some level you had a dangerous sibling, and you stayed on my good side to protect yourself."

A slight movement in her peripheral vision caught April's attention, but she kept her gaze focused on her brother, pretending to be fascinated by his words when in reality she'd grown tired of him and his confessions.

Maybe he was right. Maybe she'd always known what he was on some level. Now that his mask had completely slipped, he no longer bore any resemblance to the brother she'd tried to build up in her mind.

He'd murdered her mother. Set up her father. Tricked her into staying away from the man she loved.

While Adam opened his mouth to continue his bragging, his jaw dropped and his eyes bugged out of his skull.

The weapon in his hand wavered, and April dropped to the sand.

Clay had emerged from the tunnel like some avenging desert creature of the night, tackling Adam to the ground. Adam squeezed off a shot that pinged off the rock where she'd just been sitting.

The gun must've recoiled in his hand when he pulled the trigger because as Clay took him down, it flew from his grasp. The two men grappled on the ground, Clay clawing the sand to reach his own weapon that he'd placed just outside the cave to wrap his arms around Adam's legs and destabilize him.

Adam's wiry strength and manic energy made up for the weight and muscle difference between him and Clay. As Clay landed a punch on Adam's face, Adam squirmed out from beneath him and scrabbled for Clay's gun, shoved up against the rock.

An adrenaline rush surged through April's system and she launched herself forward, snatching up the weapon that had flown out of Adam's hand. Her weapon.

Hitching up to her knees, she swung the gun toward the two men rolling closer to the other gun, Adam's fingers stretching out for the barrel.

"Stop!" She wrenched the word from her parched throat. "Stop, now. Leave the gun, Adam."

He smiled through bleeding lips. "You're not going to do it, April. I'm your little brother."

As both Adam and Clay made a final, desperate grab for the gun, April took aim and fired.

Epilogue

April buried her face in Denali's fur, the coarse texture tickling her nose. "How's the progress on those tunnels going?"

Clay placed a glass of wine on the firepit, and the flickering reds and oranges filtered through the shimmering liquid. "We've gotten to half of them already. Some are crude, some are sophisticated, all were conduits for drugs and God knows what else for Las Moscas."

"It's a gold mine of information, isn't it?" April stretched her hand to the fire and wiggled her fingers before pinching the stem of the wineglass and taking a sip of the cold chardonnay.

"Thanks to you."

She tipped her glass in Clay's direction. "Officially, thanks to you."

"Less complicated for me to take credit for shooting and killing your brother than you." He swirled the wine in his glass. "Unless you've changed your mind."

She shoved her hair behind her ear and sniffed.

"I don't want it to be known that I killed Adam—even though he deserved it."

"Not only did he deserve it, you took the shot in self-defense. He'd abducted you at gunpoint, and if he'd reached that gun before I did, he would've killed you."

"At that moment, I didn't even think about that." She ran her fingertip around the rim of her glass. "It was you I was worried about. Always you, Clay."

He pushed up to his feet and sat next to her on the other side of the firepit in his backyard. He set down his glass and draped his arm around her shoulders. "Misplaced worry. If you had just told me two years ago that someone was threatening you, threatening us, I probably could've nipped this entire thing in the bud."

"If we'd gone through with the wedding, Adam would've killed you. I'm sure of that." She grabbed his fingers brushing her arm, and entwined hers with them. "Why didn't my parents try to get him help?"

"Maybe they just didn't recognize what he was. You didn't."

"I was a child, and he was my younger brother."

"You didn't recognize him for what he was even when you were both adults. I guess he got better at hiding the fact that he didn't have any real emotions, no human feeling."

"He's right. I didn't want to see it. Especially after Mom…died and Dad disappeared." She bolted upright. "Dad should know. He should know he's no longer a suspect in Mom's murder."

Clay stroked his hand down her back. "Maybe someday, April. If he really is El Gringo Viejo, you don't want him back in your life, anyway."

"If?" She cranked her head to the side. "You were so sure he wasn't. What changed?"

"Adam believed it with all his heart—of course, that's not saying much. Did he convince you?"

"I'm not sure. He would never tell me what evidence he had."

"You know what's curious?"

"Lots of things. What?"

"The other female mule? They ID'd her. She was an ex-pat living in Mexico, may have had connections to El Gringo Viejo."

"Which means El Gringo Viejo may be working against Las Moscas?"

"Maybe. He's Mexico's problem right now. We'll have our hands full destroying those tunnels."

"Hey, you two." Meg stood at the patio door, music floating outside from behind her. "The party's in here…or maybe not."

April waved. "We'll be there in a minute."

When Meg closed the door, Clay scooted in closer and nuzzled her hair. "Or two, or three."

Cupping his jaw, she whispered, "Have I ever told you I love you?"

"Not for a few years, but your actions speak louder than those three words ever could." He kissed her throat. "Don't ever try to protect me again without telling me about it first. Besides, that's *my* job."

"That's *our* job, together. Isn't that what's in the wedding vows?"

"I'm not sure. I never got to say those vows."

"Me, either."

"When are we going to remedy that?"

"How close is Vegas?"

"Not close enough."

And as Clay wrapped his arms around her and pressed a kiss against her willing mouth, she whispered against his lips, "Not close enough."

* * * * *

*Look for the next book in Carol Ericson's
Holding the Line miniseries when*
Chain of Custody *goes on sale in July 2020,
only from Harlequin Intrigue!*

#1935 DOUBLE ACTION DEPUTY
Cardwell Ranch: Montana Legacy • by B.J. Daniels
When Montana deputy marshal Brick Savage asks homicide detective
Maureen Mortensen to help him find the person who destroyed her family, she
quickly accepts his offer. But as the stakes rise and they get closer than they ever
expected, can they find the killer before they become targets?

#1936 RUNNING OUT OF TIME
Tactical Crime Division • by Cindi Myers
To find out who poisoned some medications, two TCD agents go undercover and
infiltrate the company posing as a married couple. But as soon as Jace Cantrell
and Laura Smith arrive at Stroud Pharmaceuticals, someone ups the ante by
planting explosives in their midst.

#1937 CHAIN OF CUSTODY
Holding the Line • by Carol Ericson
When a baby lands on border patrol agent Nash Dillon's doorstep, Emily Lang,
an undercover investigator posing as a nanny, comes to his rescue. But once he
discovers why Emily is really there—and that both her and the baby's life are in
danger—he'll unleash every skill in his arsenal to keep them out of harm's way.

#1938 BADLANDS BEWARE
A Badlands Cops Novel • by Nicole Helm
When Detective Tucker Wyatt is sent to protect Rachel Knight from her father's
enemies, neither of them realizes exactly how much danger she's in. As she starts
making connections between her father's past and a current disappearance,
she's suddenly under attack from all sides.

#1939 A DESPERATE SEARCH
An Echo Lake Novel • by Amanda Stevens
Detective Adam Thayer is devastated when he fails to save his friend. But a series
of clues brings Adam to coroner Nikki Dresden, who's eager to determine if one
of the town's most beloved citizens was murdered. They must work together to
unravel a deadly web of lies and greed...or die trying.

#1940 WITNESS ON THE RUN
by Cassie Miles
WITSEC's Alyssa Bailey is nearly attacked until investigator Rafe Fournier comes
to her defense. Even so, Alyssa is unsure of who she can trust thanks to gaps in
her memory. Racing to escape whoever has discovered her whereabouts, they
soon learn what truths hide in the past.

After very little sleep and an early call from his father the next morning, Brick dressed in his uniform and drove down to the law enforcement building. He was hoping that this would be the day that his father, Marshal Hud Savage, told him he would finally be on active duty. He couldn't wait to get his teeth into something, a real investigation. After finding that woman last night, he wanted more than anything to be the one to get her justice.

"Come in and close the door," his father said before motioning him into a chair across from his desk.

"Is this about the woman I encountered last night?" he asked as he removed his Stetson and dropped into a chair across from his father. He'd stayed at the hospital until the doctor had sent him home. When he called this morning, he'd been told that the woman appeared to be in a catatonic state and was unresponsive.

"We have a name on your Jane Doe," his father said now. "Natalie Berkshire."

Brick frowned. The name sounded vaguely familiar. But that wasn't what surprised him. "Already? Her fingerprints?"

Hud nodded and slid a copy of the *Billings Gazette* toward him. He picked it up and saw the headline sprawled across the front page, "Alleged Infant Killer Released for Lack of Evidence." The newspaper was two weeks old.

Brick felt a jolt rock him back in his chair. "She's that woman?" He couldn't help his shock. He thought of the terrified woman who'd crossed in front of his truck last night. She was nothing like the woman he remembered seeing on television coming out of the law enforcement building in Billings after being released.

"I don't know what to say." Nor did he know what to think. The woman he'd found had definitely been victimized. He thought he'd saved her. He'd been hell-bent on getting her justice. With his Stetson balanced on his knee, he raked his fingers through his hair.

"I'm trying to make sense of this, as well," his father said. "Since her release, more evidence had come out in former cases. She's now wanted for questioning in more deaths of patients who'd been under her care from not just Montana. Apparently, the moment she was released, she disappeared. Billings PD checked her apartment. It appeared that she'd left in a hurry and hasn't been seen since."

"Until last night when she stumbled in front of my pickup," Brick said. "You think she's been held captive all this time?"

"Looks that way," Hud said. "We found her older-model sedan parked behind the convenience store down on Highway 191. We're assuming she'd stopped for gas. The attendant who was on duty recognized her from a photo. She remembered seeing Natalie at the gas pumps and thinking she looked familiar but couldn't place her at the time. The attendant said a large motor home pulled in and she lost sight of her and didn't see her again."

"When was this?" Brick asked.

"Two weeks ago. Both the back seat and the trunk of her car were full of her belongings."

"So she was running away when she was abducted." Brick couldn't really blame her. "After all the bad publicity, I can see where she couldn't stay in Billings. But taking off like that makes her either look guilty—or scared."

"Or both."

Don't miss
Double Action Deputy *by B.J. Daniels,*
available July 2020 wherever
Harlequin Intrigue books and ebooks are sold.

Harlequin.com

HIEXP0620